CONTEMPORARY AMERICAN FICTION

LEAVING BROOKLYN

The author of *Rough Strife*, *Disturbances in the Field*, and *The Melting Pot and Other Subversive Stories*, Lynne Sharon Schwartz lives in New York City.

LYNNE SHARON SCHWARTZ

LEAVING BROOKLYN

PENGUIN BOOKS

Just when he was starting to be interesting, to sound almost like a book, I would have to leave him. And he accepted that so easily. I had prepared, steeled myself as if with a girdle from the lingerie shop window, to hear more wild words. But he wasn't talking about drowning in desire or running away; he was thinking of getting tea bags and aspirins for Helene on the way home. Our talk reeked of finality — otherwise we wouldn't have talked at all. As scary as the mad words had been, this was worse. Quite safe.

"If you feel it's so wrong," I said, "why do you do it?"

"I told you why last time. I didn't think you wanted to hear it again. Why do you do it? Do you know?"

"But I don't feel so guilty. I'm not losing sleep over this."

"No? You must wonder something about it."

"Well, yes, I do." I frightened myself, speaking so candidly. I was never so candid with anyone in Brooklyn, and besides that, he was a grown man.

He put his hand on my stomach. He moved it down till it covered all the hair and rested it there, cupping the pubic bone. "Well, what?" He pressed down as though to encourage me, or push an answer out of me.

"All right. What you see in me, really. Since you hardly know anything about me. That's what I don't get."

"Audrey," he said soberly, "you are painfully amusing."

My eyes filled with tears. "I thought," I whispered, "you would give me an answer."

He kissed me and began caressing me again, murmuring in my ear that he loved me. I was confused. I had thought that part was over. And he had never said it like that, calmly. Perhaps I was supposed to say, I love you too, but — God, the purity of her! — I would have had to figure out first whether, in any sense of the word, I did love him, and there was no time for figuring.

"Turn over," he said softly.

He wanted that. Well. Of all the ways, this was not the most pleasurable — I couldn't come unless he reached around to touch me with his fingers — but it gave another sort of

PENGUIN BOOKS
Published by the Penguin Group
Viking Penguin, a division of Penguin Books USA Inc.,
375 Hudson Street, New York, New York 10014, U.S.A.
Penguin Books Ltd, 27 Wrights Lane,
London W8 5TZ, England
Penguin Books Australia Ltd, Ringwood,
Victoria, Australia
Penguin Books Canada Ltd, 2801 John Street,
Markham, Ontario, Canada L3R 1B4
Penguin Books (N.Z.) Ltd, 182–190 Wairau Road,
Auckland 10, New Zealand

Penguin Books Ltd, Registered Offices:
Harmondsworth, Middlesex, England

First published in the United States of America by
Houghton Mifflin Company, 1989
Published in Penguin Books 1990

1   3   5   7   9   10   8   6   4   2

Lines from "The Road Not Taken," by Robert Frost, copyright 1916 by Holt, Rinehart and Winston and renewed 1944 by Robert Frost. Reprinted from *The Poetry of Robert Frost,* edited by Edward Connery Lathem, by permission of Henry Holt and Company, Inc. Lines from "What Is This Gypsy Passion for Separation?" by Marina Tsvetayeva, from *Selected Poems of Marina Tsvetayeva,* translated by Elaine Feinstein, copyright © 1971, 1981 by Elaine Feinstein. Reprinted by permission of the publisher, E. P. Dutton, a division of NAL Penguin Inc.

LIBRARY OF CONGRESS CATALOGING IN PUBLICATION DATA
Schwartz, Lynne Sharon.
Leaving Brooklyn/Lynne Sharon Schwartz.
p.   cm.
ISBN 0 14 01.3197 3
I. Title.
[PS3569.C567L4   1990]
813'.54—dc20   89–78364

Printed in the United States of America

He who sees the Infinite in all things sees
God. He who sees the Ratio only sees
himself only.

— WILLIAM BLAKE

LEAVING
BROOKLYN

This is the story of an eye, and how it came into its own.

"You were perfect when you first came out," my mother insisted. But between the moment of my birth and her next inspection I suffered an injury to my right eye. How it occurred is a mystery. Some blunder made in handling was all she would murmur — drops, doctors, nurses, vagueness: "These things happen."

My mother probably didn't know the details of the eye injury — if it was an injury — for it would have been sacrilege for her to have questioned a doctor at that time and in that place, Brooklyn on the eve of war, a locus of customs and mythologies as arbitrary and rooted as in the Trobriand Islands or the great Aztec city of Teotihuacán where ritual sacrifices were performed monthly, the victims' blood coursing down the steps of the great Pyramid of the Sun. In comparison, my damage was minor.

Her vagueness still puzzled me, though, because her favorite retort, when she suspected me of lying, was "To thine own self be true." As it happened, lying was not my style; I leaned more towards omission. But she was canny; she knew when something was missing or out of kilter. So did I, and so I found her phrase suspicious. "To thine own self be true," on her lips, meant that though I might persist in lying to her, I had better be honest with myself. Yet she used it to pry out the truth, the whole truth. Shouldn't she have investigated the matter of the eye, likewise, to be true to herself?

("Not *she*. Don't call her she," I can already hear my father interrupting, not understanding that the "she" is a form of warlike intimacy, referring to someone so close she doesn't require a noun, someone on the embattled ground between first and third person, self and other. "Call her your mother." Very well, my mother.)

Only much later did I find that those words referred to quite a different sort of fidelity, to not bending your identity out of shape to fit the fashion. But by that time I was light years out of Brooklyn. I was becoming an actress. I was playing Polonius's daughter.

I never broached the subject with my father, such matters not being, as he might put it, in his "department." Also, he needed to be right in everything he undertook, and bristled at any hint of error or bungling. His department covered money and cars and going to work. I knew about the money part, for as far back as I could remember he would sit down after dinner at his small desk in the dining room, a desk that looked almost too small for him to fit his knees under, and I would stand beside him, jiggling the metal handles on the drawers, wordless but beseeching, till he pulled me up onto his lap. With arms reaching around me, he would go through mail, tear open envelopes, leaf through papers, and write. What was he doing?

He explained what bills were. "You should pay a bill the same day you receive it. Why wait?"

He would write out a check in his gallant, illegible writing — so that forever after I considered illegible writing a sign of masculinity and sophistication — put it in a small white envelope, dart his tongue across the wide V of the flap, pound it shut on the desk with his fist — the vibrations thumped excitedly through my body — and affix a stamp. Then he would tear up the remaining bits of paper littering the desk. Once in a while he even tore up an envelope unopened. He tore it across, then tore two or three more times with fierce gusts of energy, and threw the scraps in the wastebasket under the desk.

"Why do you have to tear it up?"

"It's garbage."

"I know, but why do you have to tear it up? Why can't you just throw it away?"

He looked at me in startled, confused pleasure, as if I had cunningly put my finger on one of the profound and inexplicable contradictions at the heart of things, as if I had asked why is there suffering in the world or why do men constantly make war if they say they want peace. He tousled my hair and had no answer, which surprised me because he usually did.

I minded the mystery of the eye more than the eye itself. I craved an exotic story to tell, a label by which I might be known. At school there was Carlotta Kaplowitz, famed for her dark beauty and wondrous name — one of the few girls not named Barbara or Susan or Carol or Judy — who contracted polio. When she returned months later on crutches, scattering true medical tales like favors, she was lionized in the playground. Polio was dramatic, though Carlotta's case, like Hans Castorp's tuberculosis, was mild — she would walk again. Another girl, one of the Carols, stayed home for a whole term with an unnamed ailment. I brought her the class assignments. How enviously I breathed the musty, invalid air of the shaded room where she sat propped up on pillows, her every need attended to by her scurrying mother, like a Victorian heroine enervated by vocation, like Elizabeth Barrett before she met Browning.

The iris of my right eye was smaller than that of the left. And at the top of the sphere, the part you couldn't see unless the lid was raised, was a milky, blurry patch, a scar. It was as if someone had painted an eye and smudged the upper rim, giving it an unfinished look, then was called away from the easel — an emergency, a long trip — and never came back.

The smudging was not all. Because of a weak muscle, the iris, of its own volition and at unpredictable times, would drift from its resting place to float — I almost wrote "flee" — beneath the upper lid for a few seconds, leaving blank white space. A wandering eye, it is aptly called. Restless, bored with the banality of what is presented, it escapes to the private darkness beneath the lid, with the wild dancing colors. Soon it drifts back and attends to its duties, not being totally irresponsible. Much of the time no one would know about its little trip, just as no one knows about the secret journeys or aberrations of anyone else.

The eye was of scant use in seeing what had to be seen in daily life in Brooklyn. It was made for another sort of vision. By legal standards it was a blind eye, yet it did see in its idiosyncratic way — shapes and colors and motion, all in their true configurations except all turned to fuzz. Its world was a Seurat painting, with the bonds hooking the molecules all severed, so that no object really cohered; the separate atoms were lined up next to one another, their union voluntary, not fated. This made the world, through my right eye, a tenuous place where the common, reasonable laws of physics did not apply, where a piece of face or the leg of a table or frame of a window might at any moment break off and drift away. I could tease and tempt the world, squinting my left eye shut and watching things disintegrate, and when I was alone my delight was to play with the visible world this way, breaking it down and putting it back together. I had secret vision and knowledge of the components of things, of the volatile nature of things before they congeal, of the tenuousness and vulnerability of all things, unknown to those with common binary vision who saw the world of a piece, with a seamless skin like the skin of a sausage holding things together. My right eye removed the skin of the visible world.

And so the girl I was, the girl I would like to reincarnate here, possessed double vision. Not simultaneous. Alternate. Her world was veiled and then, when she shut the ordinary eye and allowed the other free play, it was unveiled; the act of learning anything was not absorbing or digging out or encountering, but removing a veil, and it was the most dramatic act imaginable. From the start she had a taste for drama, self-dramatization, and her themes, naturally, were secrecy and hiding and revelation, the doling out and manipulation of information. She thought that she too could be unveiled in similar fashion, that like an ocean, she was surface and depths, and she feared this unveiling without knowing what would be revealed or why it might be dangerous. Perhaps it was simply the secret of her double vision that she feared would be exposed, for as her childhood moved along its dual paths she sensed she wasn't supposed to be seeing what she saw.

I still see as she saw. With all the advances of optics they have never found a way to fuse the two worlds. As I approached middle age I needed the usual reading glasses: my left eye got a mild prescription for aging eyes. For my right eye, nothing but window glass. That rebel eye refused to be corrected. It clung to what it had seen for her and done for her from the start.

Telling about her is an attempt at unveiling her, an act of self-sabotage, if one assumes that the woman I am today is that girl worked over and layered by time. The common wisdom holds that the process of growing older involves a toughening of the skin. But it may be the opposite, a gradual removal of layers, a peeling process. The girl has been stripped by time to produce me. I suspect I was there all along, though she is so very tough and layered that when I focus my vision to see her I can scarcely glimpse myself beneath. Before she vanishes altogether from memory — for even now memory threatens to be more invention than recall — I want to make her transparent. I want to expose the mystery of change and recall, peel her story off her the way some people can peel an orange, in one exquisite unbroken spiral.

▭

My mother opened the broiler door and orange and blue flames leaped out. Inside was a chicken we had bought that afternoon from the chicken man on Rutland Road, whose son, Bobby, off fighting the war, was my secret love.

"Oh my God," cried my mother, and she ran to the sink and filled a glass with water.

At last. Something was happening in Brooklyn, our remote little outpost. I put down the *Reader's Digest* and watched as though it were a Technicolor movie. My mother poured the water on the flames, which made them leap higher and glow more orange. They brightened, they sizzled and cavorted. She watered the fire and it grew like an overwrought plant.

My father ran in from the back porch where he was smoking his cigar in the early spring evening, kicked the broiler door shut, and turned off the oven. A few bluish-green flames oozed from the crevices. My mother stood gasping, rubbing her hands up and down her flowered apron, as the escaping flames dwindled to smoke and the rancid smell of drowned grease filled the kitchen. After a moment or two my father bent and cautiously opened the door. The flames were still alive but sizzled in a more docile way. He poured a pot of water over the chicken, and there was a weak dreary noise, a dying sputter. The fire was quenched.

I waited for some sarcastic insult to come from my father's lips, for he was compelled to insult people at moments of crisis. But he was so shocked he could not say a word, only glare. His face darkened. A muscle in his neck started twitching.

"I couldn't help it," said my mother. "When I heard it on the radio I was so upset I forgot all about the chicken."

Roosevelt was dead.

This, I knew, had something to do with the war.

My earliest years were years of wartime. Someone born elsewhere and writing those words might be recalling carnage and deprivation. At college a student older than I read aloud a personal essay about trudging along a road leading out of Dresden, the bloody bodies of people and horses sprawled in her path. I had never seen a bloody body, not even an ordinary dead one; her essay made me feel innocent, criminally innocent. Earlier, in an acting class I took when I was fifteen, I saw branded on the forearm of a pale girl a many-digited number two and a half inches above the wrist. I had known the girl through the fall and winter, but only in the spring when we wore short-sleeved blouses did the number show itself. I knew it for exactly what it was, though in Brooklyn we never spoke of those details of the war and I did not read the papers much. It was something one knew, that was all, like competition and death. I felt a twinge of envy between my ribs and was immediately ashamed and horrified, for we were trained, in Brooklyn, to feel shame at every wayward emotion, but I forgive her now, that girl I was. She was ignorant and impoverished. I didn't covet the other girl's suffering, only her knowledge; I wished it were possible to have the one without the other.

The immigrants and children of immigrants who settled Brooklyn did so precisely to shield their children from carnage and deprivation and numbers, both the suffering of them and the knowledge: they chose their place and shored it up as a fortress. They were very successful, and it would be naïve to disparage their success out of lethal nostalgia for sufferings never suffered. But perhaps only such a fortress could produce that particular vanity, the vanity of craving a more elevated position in the hierarchy of pain.

My war in Brooklyn was three things: the departure of Bobby; the ration lines in the basement of the building that would be my school when I was old enough to go to school, where I stood at my mother's right side holding her hand and waiting for our turn; and the wires on the milk bottles. The milk came in thick glass bottles left in an unpainted wooden box on our front porch in the early hours by someone we never saw but communicated with by notes left in the box. Cream gathered at the top of the bottles and caked the inside neck with a thick ring. Before opening a bottle of milk, my mother shook it up and down with swift twists of the wrist. Then she carefully unwound the thin metal wire holding the paper cap in place, a cap meticulously fluted at the lower edge like the paper booties wrapped around the bones of lamb chops in the Coney Island restaurants where we often drove for Sunday dinner. She saved the wire for the war, putting it in a drawer near the kitchen sink. Every so often my father would carry off the accumulated wires to some mysterious place, the headquarters of the war, where, he said, they were used to make things that helped our soldiers fight. Fight who? I asked. Hitler, he said, in such a way that I couldn't tell if it was the name of a person or an army or a country or a monster. He muttered the word fast, as if he were speaking not to me but to ominous enemies crouched in the air, as if it were a perilous magic word that might rot his teeth or sear his tongue if he said it too loud or let it linger too long in his mouth.

With all my mother's shaking, a ring of cream still clung to the neck of the bottle; it could not be fully homogenized by hand. Even after milk arrived homogenized, it was a long time before I lost the habit of shaking it as my mother had done. Thus do our parents cheat mortality, for a while.

Roosevelt was succeeded by Harry Truman. Who the hell was he? my father sneered, just a haberdasher from Missouri who played the piano. I asked what a haberdasher was — it sounded like something thrilling, a swashbuckling pirate or an explorer who sailed the seven seas — and he told me. So Truman was like Charlie of Cheap Charlie's Bargain Store on Rutland Road, where underwear and pyjamas and socks were piled on tables and women fingered them while children like me waited alongside, melting in a kind of boredom endemic to childhood and to Brooklyn, waiting for our lives to begin. Charlie was a tall, gray, stooped, soft-spoken man who always knew what underwear would fit whom. Our President was just like a man in Brooklyn, and I shared my father's dismay. But in time my father felt better about Truman. In time Truman even ended the war.

We were away in the mountains then, for the better air and different neighbors, though in essence the neighbors were not so different from our city neighbors, merely possessed of different faces and bodies: they moved and spoke in a more relaxed mode, gentler and more affable, like the air.

We celebrated with a great parade down the dirt roads on a sunlit August evening. My mother was the leader, prancing and banging a tambourine that she had obtained I knew not where, and I, as always, marched at her side — her right side. It was easier for me to see people on my left. I had almost no peripheral vision on the right and had to turn my head in order to see. I was not conscious of arranging myself that way; it happened.

Behind us stretched a long line of mostly women and children — the men worked in the city and came up on weekends. My mother had the tambourine and the rest of us banged pots and pans with spoons, singing "You're a Grand Old Flag," and new paraders joined us from cottages along the way.

It was a thrill to be walking freely along the dirt road where normally I was not permitted to venture alone, and the only unlovely part was the cakes of cow dung we stepped over, which I used to think were chocolate cakes until my father enlightened me. I had asked, during a twilight walk, why there were so many chocolate cakes in the road, and he replied with a laugh, "Do you want to bring one home for dinner?" I was puzzled. He told me the cows made them and I was mortified.

I noticed that one woman, the wife of the farmer whose farm we were staying at, was not part of our parade.

"Why?" I asked my mother.

"She lost her son. She doesn't have the heart for it."

I pictured her son gone astray in the dark, a boy around my age — six — who had wandered off down the forbidden road or into the woods, while his mother waited anxiously for him to turn up. Then, in the instantaneous way that children grasp the meanings of words, some convulsive juncture of ganglia in the brain, I understood. I had a million questions about him, this victim of the war, but I said nothing amid the jangle of pots and pans and tambourine.

As twilight descended the paraders lit torches that flamed in the enveloping shadows, to light the way, I thought, for the returning heroes.

We were passing a scruffy field where a black dog flecked with auburn circled a gray terrier who stood still and meditative. After a moment he climbed on her back, balancing on his hind legs.

The woman parading on the other side of my mother poked her and nodded in the direction of the dogs. "Also celebrating."

"And why not?" my mother answered, and the two of them grinned.

The black dog, poised over the terrier, jerked his body a few times while his partner gazed about with her meditative air, as though nothing were happening. Then he pulled away, and both dogs went trotting off in the weeds, separately, and our parade passed on.

"How did the war end?" I asked my mother.

She stopped banging her tambourine. "We dropped a bomb and they surrendered."

Maybe this meant Bobby would be home soon.

When I first fell in love he was sixteen, twelve years older than I, but over the few years I loved him I learned, by reading and observing couples around me, that a dozen years did not remain an uncrossable gap. Time shrank with age. When I was sixteen he would be twenty-eight, when I was twenty he would be thirty-two . . .

From as early as I can remember, until I was about twelve years old, I was always in love, though Bobby was the first and, perhaps because of the supernatural gifts of his mother, the best and longest love. Sometimes it was a boy in my class; more often it was someone older and unattainable, a friend's big brother or a boy working after school in a luncheonette, or the sons of my parents' friends. I would see them two or three times, barely speak to them, and spend the next few months talking to them in my head, telling everything I thought and dreamed, supplying their responses and gestures, inventing their characters and temperaments from the bare physical elements. So I was never alone. This being in love, in my early years, felt like a condition inherent to life, like having body temperature; or a sixth sense, an extra mode of perceiving, of extending my reach in the world and bringing it all back inside. And it never seemed strange that love was always with me, attached to someone ignorant of the attachment, or that I lived my life with an image secretly installed in my head while the original went about his life all unaware that his image dwelt with me in captivity. And then at twelve years old, just when most girls are starting, I stopped falling in love. I opened my eyes and apprehended the tangible world of bodies and boundaries, limits and mortality. I saw how absurd and illusory my being in love was. Why should I do this? How foolish to love so much, give so much in secret, and get nothing real in return. Love was not a condition of life, but an artificial corrective to the truly inherent condition of being alone. Love had disappointed me, and I broke myself of the habit of loving and gave myself to solitude.

There is no explaining these sudden and terrible conversions, but surely mine had something to do with Mrs. Amerman, the seventh-grade Social Studies teacher. "Accuracy and speed. Accuracy and speed," chanted Mrs. Amerman, training us to excel in the standardized tests that determined our school's rank in the city. "Accuracy and speed." The sort of prayer that, no matter what the political climate, is always permitted in the public schools. "Those qualities are not only for the test. They will help you get through life as well." She also taught outline form, which had a certain classic beauty and feeling of safe containment, like the gardens at Versailles, and very unlike my kind of love. The largest category was the roman numeral. Below the roman numeral came the capital letters. Below the capital letters came the arabic numerals, and below them, the lower-case letters. In case you had to subdivide further, there were the lower-case roman numerals, little *i*'s: *i, ii, iii, iv*. The headings marched down the page, each one indented farther to the right till the design on the page was an upside-down staircase. Any thought could be fit somewhere in the outline, once you figured out its degree of significance in the pattern. Above all, every single thing in the world could be outlined.

There was one major rule to remember, Mrs. Amerman warned. "You can't have a I without a II. You can't have an A without a B. It's only logical. Because nothing can be divided into one part. Do you see, children?"

I was accurate, logical, speedy. No fact escaped the net of my outlines, like wayward hairs tucked into a bun. Through high school, I took notes of the teachers' casual remarks in outline form, corralling the syllables that bounced haphazardly on the air into right-angled shapes on the pages of my notebook.

Now what I love is slowness. Slow people, slow reading, slow traveling, slow eggs, and slow love. Everything good comes slow. And inaccuracy. Things just slightly off, falling nonchalantly from perfection. Things beautiful in spite of.

And it is possible, on occasion, to subdivide into one part. The one part becomes refined and polished and narrowed, the shavings fall away, out of sight, till the kernel is exposed like a gem absorbing and reflecting the multiplicity of the world.

To tell how my eye led me down the road it did, I must say a word or two of the climatic conditions of postwar Brooklyn. The air was suspended on a discrepancy, something like the discrepancy between my mother's use of the words "To thine own self be true" and their true meaning. It was a presumption of state-of-nature innocence, an imaginative amnesia, and a disregard of evidence such as photographs of skeletal figures in striped pyjamas clawing at barbed wire, of mushroom clouds and skinned bodies groping in ashes. News of distant atmospheric pollution. The evidence was not only in newspaper photographs. The most zealous Brooklynites had themselves fled the armbands and the midnight blazes. They knew, they knew. Yet with all that furor in the air, the slogans they sent forth on placid streams of breath were simple and pure, extolling righteous endeavor, progress, and conformity, as if the pollution were illusory, only a haze veiling the reality, which was human decency. The slogans were enforced through a tacit system of mutual surveillance and with a magnificently unwarranted faith in will power, education, and the forming of proper habits. As everywhere, perhaps, children were designed and packaged to embody an "image" of human nature. What was special about Brooklyn was how ingenuously it admitted no gulf between image and reality. Now that corruption is publicly taken for granted and "image" has detached from reality to acquire independent life, every child over ten knows what Brooklyn pretended not to know.

I knew some things apart from the slogans, though, things that gnawed and nibbled away at the smug sound of them. Late at night, in bed, I read the old books my parents stored in my room, somber black Harvard Classics with gilt lettering on the bindings and green Little Leather Library books, the corners of the faded pages crumbling in my fingers and littering the blanket. I read stealthily as though the books were forbidden, just for the glamour of it — they were not forbidden, only I sensed it was the better part of valor to keep my passion secret.

After the orgies of reading, I played games with my eye. There was a way, if I closed my "good" eye, as my mother called it, and kept the bad eye open, that I could see through the edges of solid objects like pillows or doors — see the margin of what was on the other side of the door. And so I squinted and peered through the corners of my pillow to see bits of the blue and orange clowns and dancers stenciled on my wall in repeating yellow squares. I could make the figures jiggle and dissolve, and see parts that were out of range when I had both eyes open. With my good eye shut I could even see a different design of leafy branches through the casement window, and different patterns of stars, maybe the stars as they were in another time or place. I could vault out of my time and place and be somewhere else in history, in the world.

This was not pure fancy: the center of my vision was in front of my "good" left eye rather than over the bridge of my nose; it follows that my world was two inches to the left of everyone else's. But logic doesn't nullify anything, it is only a little breeze. I did have the power to glimpse what was behind things. And because these secrets were mine alone, I was greedy for them. What is politely called curiosity in children is greed. The objects of greed are shaped by what we feel we have in short supply. I was told I didn't see in the regular way, so I had to acquire special sights. I had to know what was behind everything. I had to peel whatever I saw.

If I knew something others did not, the opposite was true too. What would be forever denied me was "depth perception." I could see nothing extraordinary through the viewing machines at the top of the Empire State Building, while others gasped at the panorama. With only one eye, they told me, everything was flat and in the same plane, and therefore I was doomed to live in a flattened version of the world. This was painful to hear, and not true. I saw gradations of distance. I was a good judge of distances, a whiz at punch ball in the streets. It might be true for *them,* when they shut one eye, but I had learned to compensate. This fact an eye doctor volunteered years later, though I couldn't remember consciously learning anything of the kind. My eyes and hands and body learned. But if I had indeed invented distance and proportion for myself, who could know it better?

There was something people saw with their two eyes pressed against those machines, though, and the girl I was feared she would die without knowing what it was, because no one who had it could explain it, just as you can describe a landscape to a recently blinded person, but where are the words to explain "cloud" or "shadow" or the act of seeing them to someone blind from birth? And even if I suddenly had it, I might not recognize it or like it, just as some people blind from birth and suddenly given sight cannot make out the world at all, cannot reconcile the light and dark patches they see with their inner vision or comprehension of objects, and take weeks or months to accept the shapes and patterns of the world, or maybe never do, and live longingly in exile from their own perceptions.

Most things cannot be explained unless the listener has some prior inkling of them, which doesn't augur well for traditional forms of education. We learn what we have the nerve paths prepared to receive — grammar and justice and cause and effect for all, music or quantum physics for a few. Socrates believed his students had an innate, if dormant, grasp of the principles of geometry and logic and justice, but formal learning in Brooklyn was very far from Socratic; each student was a *tabula rasa* on which teachers doggedly inscribed four reasons for British imperialism, three reasons for the outbreak of World War I, three products of Brazil.

Whatever depth perception there was in Brooklyn was flattened by the collective will, but I couldn't know that. I knew only that I would never see depth as others saw it. And so I persistently looked for the endlessly receding, stratified planes, even in cases where there was no depth. I tried to make more out of less, even out of Brooklyn. I couldn't accept that some things remain flat no matter how hard you strain to confer dimensions on them.

I say Brooklyn with a certain acidity, though at other times I might — I do — say it with affection. The Brooklyn of my story is not the place, a rather pretty place of tender low houses and gracious trees and regal avenues, a place lapped by salt water and rich with briny air, with innumerable earthy charms, and so this cannot be a story built with the ordinary scenery of stories, furniture and interior decoration and local color. The Brooklyn of my story is a state of mind or perception, the shadow field on which my good and bad eyes staged their struggle. It could as readily be called Cleveland or Rouen or Johannesburg. It moves from place to place wherever opposing visions struggle, but unlike a shadow it never changes with the light. One can only live in it or flee.

Being in love is one kind of flight, and in the early years of my love I longed to fly to the chicken man and butcher's store to see Bobby: tall, swarthy, burly, with translucent blue eyes, dressed in black chino pants and a gray sweatshirt, an easy-mannered boy who charmed the women customers and always had a ready word for me. When I was lucky enough to find him in the store — he helped out after school hours, from four to seven — he would look up as I entered, his hands busy wrapping chickens in brown paper or doling out change, and say, "Well, if it isn't Audrey the geisha girl." He called me that because my hair was black and shiny and combed in bangs. "How's the world treating you, kiddo?" and I would feel joy in the roots of my hair.

But this could not happen if my mother did her errands in the morning. And I could not beg her to go in the afternoon. I was ashamed of the force of my longings. I knew enough of the world to know people my age were not supposed to be in love. If I said "I want to see Bobby," my mother would say "Who? The chicken man's boy? What for?", then catch on and laugh. My love was not a feeling that could or would have been ordained by my mother, who knew not only what to do in every situation, but what to feel, too, and monitored my errant feelings. "Don't feel that way," she said when I had a grievance or wound, when I was envious or petulant or sullen. Feel the way I tell you to feel; that will feel better. She knew which feelings were proper for the occasion and which must be stamped out like a brush fire or sponged away before they hardened and set. Feelings could be read on the face, and if she read an infelicitous feeling on mine she would say offhandedly, "If you keep walking around with that expression on your face it'll freeze that way," making me think that each bad feeling would last forever, iced in my cheekbones, and this edged my every transient melancholy with a braided border of eternity and hopelessness. Wrong feelings were the most terrible kind of impropriety, and it was the hardest thing in the world to know what the right ones were, according to my mother, and then try to have them. So my love for Bobby, along with so much else, had to be secret.

Sometimes my mother had so many packages to carry, or the weather was so snowy or rainy, that she would order our dinner over the phone, and on those days Bobby would appear on our doorstep. The bell — three chimes set in a niche in the wall — would ring and I would trail my mother to the door and stand half behind her, shyly, because everything was different outside the store. On our doorstep he was another Bobby, older, with a manly dignity in his pea coat and scarf. As he handed over his package he would say, "Hey, Audrey!" and maybe reach out to punch me on the shoulder, while I could not speak for strangeness.

Even on the good days — mild late afternoons — I had to undergo ordeals before reaching Bobby, like a knight per-

forming feats of valor and endurance for a kiss from his be-
loved. I accompanied my mother on her rounds, the ration
line, the six-block stretch of Rutland Road with Cheap Charlie's, the fruit man, the shoe store, endless stations of monotony, until finally we arrived at the chicken store. It was a
fairly large shop, by Rutland Road standards, Ben the butcher
occupying the right-hand side and the chicken man the left.
Their counters, about twelve feet long, were separated by a
center aisle some two yards wide, and the aisle was strewn
with sawdust, soft and fragrant, its smell edging out the rich
pungent odor of raw poultry. Ben the butcher was a big,
dark, red-faced man who seemed kin to the slabs of raw meat
arrayed before him, and in fact Bobby resembled Ben more
than he did his own father, who was small, wiry, and fair-
haired, with a mustache and white apron and cap. The chicken
man would display his wares for my mother, chickens complete with grayish feathers and bright yellow feet and toes
and curved witches' toenails. Fresh-killed, the sign outside
said. He expounded on their virtues as my mother scruti-
nized them; meanwhile Bobby winked at me, and if he was
not busy, came from behind the counter to talk, crouching
down so that he was my size. He told me to watch out for
Mrs. Bluestone when I reached second grade, but he wouldn't
tell me what she did. He taught me how to play tic-tac-toe
and showed me little round plastic discs where the trick was
to make tiny ball bearings roll into the eye and mouth holes
punched in a clown's face, and once in a while he bought me
a Dixie cup at the candy store next door, holding my hand
as we walked. If he grabbed my right hand I would pull away
and go around him to be on his right.

When my mother had chosen a chicken, the chicken man
brought it to his wife in her special corner. This was the best
part. For the glory of Bobby was not simply in himself; it
was in his having this creature for a mother.

She sat on a folding chair at the back of the store, beside a
large wooden bin. In winter she wore layers of fuzzy shawls

in drab colors, while in summer her arms were bare, and in all seasons she wore a kerchief on her head and her house-dress was covered by a broad white apron. She sat with both feet solidly on the floor, wide apart, in black high-laced boots. She smiled but almost never spoke. When she did speak, the sounds were garbled, as if they came from an animal strug-gling to speak, yet they were close enough to human speech to be familiar and frightening. The struggling sounds were all vowels, wild and overflowing the boundaries of conso-nants; the consonants pursued the vowels to trap and tame them, but the vowels were headstrong and couldn't be caught.

This, my mother explained in the special tone of Brooklyn "tolerance," was because Bobby's mother had a cleft palate. She was not stupid, my mother said, and I must not be afraid of her; she understood everything we said to her and had thoughts and answers in her mind exactly like everyone else, but it was hard for her to make the words. And I, who so often felt impelled to speak, to hear what I knew made real and given shape in undulations of sound, and equally often regretted the words coursing out uncontrolled, regarded the woman's silence as a wondrous talent, like riding a unicycle or spinning straw into gold. She did not need to give speech to the voice inside. It was sufficient that she herself knew and heard it within. Her silence was part of her power.

But it was the lesser part. More miraculous was what she did. She was a chicken flicker, and although my father used this term to denote a person on the lowest social rung, to me she was queenly in her dominion. She reached out to accept the chicken from her husband and the spectacle began. With fervor, absorbed in her task, she pulled the feathers from the chicken, her fingers so swift that they dissolved in a blur like the blades of a propeller as they dug into the skin and released little puffs of feathers. She got faster and faster as she went along, turning the chicken around in her hands, the chicken that was growing a larger and larger bald yellow patch. Feathers flew, tossed up by the energy in her fingers, and for a brilliant instant rested poised in the air, then changed direction and made their descent. Feathers drifted through the air around her, wafting down to her lap or her boots, or to the floor. The air was dappled with flying feathers, gray and white, a little snowstorm, while the chicken flicker sat in the midst of them, large, solid, and draped, a Madonna assumed into a cloud.

Sometimes my mother, who was friendly and spoke to people in stores, especially and deliberately to those she considered less fortunate, would talk to the chicken flicker as she worked, about household or neighborhood matters. I wished she wouldn't. Her talking distracted me from the vision of the feathers and the transforming chicken and the woman with the astonishing fingers who was another order of being, a wizard absorbed in her wizardly task, while my mother was stuck in the daily quicksand of Brooklyn. And because the chicken flicker couldn't speak, I felt something unfair about my mother's chattering to her — as if speech demanded a response and my mother was demanding something the chicken flicker could not give. But speech does not always demand a response. Speech can be a simple gift, no strings attached, and no doubt that was what my mother offered. I was the one who wished to ration and dole out and barter speech.

Somewhere, someone today must pull the feathers off chickens, or more likely it is done by machine, but either way, it is not done where I can see it. Had I not watched the chicken flicker at her work I might almost believe chickens come in naked yellow skins, the only hint that they do not being the tiny holes along the surface and the occasional stump of quill you find, that escaped the machine.

Right after Bobby graduated from high school he vanished. I didn't even have a chance to say good-bye: our connection was not sanctified by any institution like romance or family; it was purely in my mind. Like famous literary adulterers, like poor foolish John Marcher of "The Beast in the

Jungle," who had no special status at the funeral of the person closest to his heart, I stood apart from the vicissitudes of Bobby's life. Mine was a love outside the social structure, that dared not speak its name.

"Where's Bobby?" I asked the chicken man one day, made bold by desperation.

"Bobby's in the Navy, sweetheart. He's away on a big ship."

I knew immediately this was part of the war. And I thought:

> Bobby Shaftoe's gone to sea
> Silver buckles on his knee
> He'll come back and marry me
> Pretty Bobby Shaftoe.

The role of waiting at home was an acid impatience. Stinging as if my blood were laced with vinegar, I dreamed of flying off to join him, stowing away on the ship. I had read of stowaways: often they were accepted by the crew after the first shock of their presence passed. I would make myself useful and become a kind of mascot. When the ship put into port I would see all sorts of glamorous places, and maybe Bobby and I would like one so much that we would never come home.

I wrote Bobby a letter telling him I had started first grade and had to sit quietly at my desk while the others learned to read, and I asked him about his ship. In my mind, as always, I told him how things truly were and felt. I told him about the somersault in my gut after the first few days of school, that sick flip I later came to recognize as meaning: Aha, so *this* is what it will be like. School was lining up in a chalk-drawn rectangle, one for each class, in the chill mornings, being forced to hold a partner's damp woollen mitten, and waiting, in the dismal silence imposed by the sixth-grade Guard Force — identified by their white strap running diagonally from shoulder to waist — for a bell to allow us in; it meant the patrolled march to the classroom, where the morning proceeded inevitably and without variation: roll call, pledge of allegiance, reading aloud in turns, milk at ten-thirty sharp, enforced rest — arms folded on the desk, heads down — the trek downstairs to the bathrooms, where the teacher handed us in pairs to the matron, a mammoth dressed in white. Recess. Forced play.

"Oh, you'll get used to it," my mother said.

I suspected — it sounds uncanny, I know, but I truly had the ghastly presentiment, at six years old — that all of life could be this way, sick with rote, and I no longer envied grownups their freedom. All this I told Bobby as I lay in bed at night dreading the morning, but I could not yet write well enough to put it in my letter.

Later on I told him, silently, in bed at night, about the eye tests. The teacher hung an eye chart over the map of the world and each child came forward, covered one eye, then the other, and read the letters on the chart. Those few with glasses got to do it twice, with and without. It was no use trying to memorize the chart, because the teacher aimed her pointer at random. My turn came. I covered my right eye and read everything she pointed to, down to the tiniest letters at the very bottom.

"All right, cover the other eye now."

The chart was still there, pulsing in the distance, and the chubby figure of Miss Tilford next to it, amorphous, threatening to shatter into its molecular components at any instant. The watery broken line must be her pointer. It shook and shimmied.

"Well, Audrey?"

"I don't know."

The pointer danced up in the direction of a dark, thick squiggle, probably the E. But since I couldn't make it out, I didn't say.

"Can't you even see this big one?"

Around me hung a taut energy. Not the mumbles and giggles that greeted the nearsighted children who fumbled through a line or two and gave up, like dummies who couldn't read. Only a stunned awe. I could barely distinguish my classmates, grainy faces in the crowd of an antique photo, but I could feel their attention seeping passionately into my skin like raw sun. I was special. With one eye I saw everything and with the other, nothing.

"Audrey, come up to my desk before you go home for lunch. I want to give you a note for your mother. You can sit down now."

My mother wouldn't tell me what was in the note. "It's all right," she said in a consoling way. "You won't have to take the test again." And she gave me a note to bring back to the teacher, and it was true, I never took the test again.

My letter to Bobby was not much, compared to these stifled intensities, a mere few lines. My mother approved of cheering up our fighting men, and said if we put the letter in an envelope with a stamp and gave it to Bobby's father, he would send it to him. She asked to read it and I said no. To emphasize my refusal I sealed it in her presence and held on to it until we next went to the chicken store.

During the three years Bobby was away I had small flurries of attachment here and there, but I kept my love for him sealed, intact. I knew there was a chance he would not return. That was what war meant: boys left home to fight and sometimes didn't come back, which was why people dreaded it, though this had not happened to anyone I knew in Brooklyn, only to the farm woman who had lost her son and didn't have the heart to march in our parade. But I knew too that the war was over — the parade had taken place shortly after Bobby joined the Navy — so probably he was not really fighting but simply sailing here and there, keeping things in order.

Now there was another war, without fighting, called the cold war. When I was seven, I saw a picture illustrating an adventure story in *The Saturday Evening Post,* which I read regularly, along with the other magazines my family received in the mail: *Redbook, The Ladies' Home Journal* ("Can This Marriage Be Saved?" — yes, almost always by the wife's learning to be more "tolerant"), *McCall's,* and *Reader's Digest* ("Life in These United States" — what a quirky, home-spun, bumbling, lovable bunch we were, for a major power). The picture showed an American spy captured in a communist country, sitting on a stool in a cellar room with his hands tied behind him, surrounded by his tormentors, the communists. The American has a tin bucket over his head. The communists batter on the bucket with sticks to break his will. That was the nature of the cold war. I never dreaded this happening to Bobby. It was nearer, already happening to me.

The image sprouted needles and tattooed itself on my brain. I lived inside a bucket of sorts, blind darkness of a sort, too, even if the living conditions were infinitely gentler. Maybe too much gentler, you may feel, for me to venture the comparison. I suppose it would only weaken my story to claim a misery or repression greater than seems warranted. Granted, then, that on the scale of brutalities Brooklyn occupied a most humble, far from epic, place. Even its repressions were humble, which made them all the more difficult to locate. Nonetheless in the hazy moments before sleep, I saw the velvety black inside of the bucket and felt the pounding of the sticks, arrhythmic, chaotic, resounding through the hollows of my skull. And I read. The sticks, such as they were, padded, nudging little sticks, tried to pound my brain into a more rudimentary state, to break the truths in the books into dusty lies. Reading was resistance, and resistance, too, was not telling what I knew.

Bobby returned. With no warning, there he was in his father's store one afternoon. Changed, resplendent in his uniform, a sailor suit identical with the ones some boys in my third-grade class wore — navy blue, a big square collar with three rows of white ribbing at the edges, and bell-bottom trousers just as the song on the radio said:

Bell-bottom trousers
Coat of navy blue
I love a sailor
And he loves me too.

"Hi there, Audrey. Thanks for the great letter." He smiled, but something was different. I was too surprised to feel what was happening, but I filmed it all with my bad eye — my storehouse of visual memory — so I could relive it later and feel its meaning. He picked me up and swung me around in the air. From the low, tentative arc of the swing, I could tell I was heavier than he had expected. How I'd grown, he said. No baby anymore. He put his white sailor hat on my head, and his wordless mother, in a whirl of feathers at the back of the store, laughed open-mouthed at the sight. I tried to persuade myself that everything would be the same as before, but in my heart I knew better. Bobby had sailed halfway across the world, far far from Brooklyn, to places whose names I didn't even know, where people dressed in sarongs and lounged under palm trees and lived in grass huts under amber skies, maybe banging drums and painting their bodies and dancing the night through with savage ecstatic wails. How small and dull and insignificant everything here must seem. What could I offer him? How could my stories of class trips to the Botanic Garden or the Prospect Park Zoo, where we giggled at the purple-bottomed apes climbing over one another, compare with the exotic things he had witnessed? Could it matter to him that I knew all about Mrs. Bluestone now? For the secret was this: each morning Mrs. Bluestone made the entire class line up at the front of the room for inspection, boys on one side and girls on the other, and examined each person's hair, ears, teeth, fingernails, shoes, and handkerchief. She made us hold our collars open to show our necks as she moved slowly down the lines, peering at each neck to judge if it was properly washed. I had told my mother Mrs. Bluestone was crazy. She was amused and said, "Oh, don't feel that way. It's silly, but it can't do any harm." Then she thought it over and added, "She's the teacher, maybe she knows what she's doing. Maybe some children aren't kept clean." So I made an effort to be amused and philosophical too, and the effort entwined with my true feelings of outrage to form a tight knot in my head. Bobby, had I told him, would have laughed his clear, straight laugh at how nothing ever changed in school, and it would have been plain that Mrs. Bluestone's way need not be the way of the world; my knot would have dissolved in laughter too. But I didn't tell him: I was ashamed that, inexplicably, my fate was to endure Mrs. Bluestone's obsessions while his was to sail the seven seas in a splendid uniform.

Soon my mother began sending me on errands. I would wait in the chicken store as all the women did while the chicken was flicked, and pay Bobby, who had become brooding, almost dour. He was never rude to me, only there seemed to be nothing special between us.

Even worse were the snowy days when he delivered the order and my mother sent me to the door. "Give Bobby half a dollar," and I had the agony of handing him his tip, which he accepted politely, thanking me as though I were just another grown and distant woman.

How could so much feeling and connection dissipate? Where in the universe did it go?

Bobby continued working for his father and married a girl he had known in high school. He got an apartment in the neighborhood, becoming one more Brooklyn person, and this was a great mystery to me — that he could have gone so far on his ship and seen so many things, only to return and marry Barbara, also called Bobby, so that one of the local jokes was Bobby and Bobby. Whenever I saw him I felt a vague awkwardness on his behalf: how ashamed and disappointed he must be, I imagined, that this was his life.

Things did not grow easier for us — for me — until I was thirteen years old and drifted into the store to buy my mother lamb chops. I waved at Bobby and turned towards Ben's side to place my order.

"Hey, Audrey, come here. You've got to see this."

He wiped his hands on his apron, pulled a wallet from the back pocket of his chinos, and showed me pictures of his baby, three weeks old: naked on its stomach, wrapped in a blanket, Barbara holding it, and Barbara and Bobby holding it, the three faces squeezed together. "How do you like that? Chip off the old block, isn't he?"

"Oh, he's a beautiful baby, Bobby," I said as I had often heard my mother do. "Really beautiful. Congratulations."

"Yeah. I'll tell you, it's a great feeling. A great feeling."

I looked at him tenderly. There was no awkwardness left, and no danger of anyone's detecting improper feelings, for I was through with unrequited soulful love. I was planning to live an exotic life in some distant, turbulent place as soon as I could, Paris maybe, attending the Sorbonne, or Cairo, where, rumor had it, if you sat in a certain café eventually everyone in the world would pass by. Maybe not people from Brooklyn, but everyone else. I marveled that I could ever have given my heart and soul to Bobby. He rumpled my hair as he hadn't done for years, and I tried not to shrink away. I saw that connections could dissolve and seemingly come to nothing, though they might be reabsorbed and reshaped to be used somewhere else in the world, a conservation of emotion like the conservation of matter or energy — the sort of open, un-regulated process my bad eye would comprehend. I squinted my good eye and Bobby merged into the chicken store, his molecules mingling with the molecules of the display cases and the paneled walls and the sawdust.

"So who do you have for History?" he asked. "Did you get Kuznetzov?"

"Oh yes," I groaned.

"You have my sympathy. Is she still torturing people in class?"

"Almost every day, I swear. She makes strong men weep when they haven't done the homework. But her main thing is communism. She doesn't let anyone open or close loose-leaf rings in class because it can lead to communism."

"How's that?"

"Clicking the rings creates excessive noise, excessive noise leads to chaos, and chaos leads to communism. I think she's actually a spy for McCarthy."

Bobby was appreciative, as always. Five years ago his response would have sustained me for days and generated a lengthy fantasy culminating in declarations of eternal love and affinity. Now I just laughed along with him. Ordinary life, nothing to embroider with dreams on the way home. I was ready to go, I had my mother's lamb chops, but he kept me. To think there could come a time when I would want to leave Bobby!

"Who do you have for Geometry? Did you get Califano? He really had a thing for the girls. He'd go for you in a big way, Audrey."

"No, I have Schechter."

"I don't remember him."

"Her. It's just as well. See you, Bobby. Have fun with the baby."

I had a secret this time, about Miss Schechter, like his about Mrs. Bluestone. But it was a secret tacitly guarded by the ninth-grade girls — I could never have told Bobby.

Before I left I went over to his mother to congratulate her on her new grandchild. She smiled and nodded vigorously and made some laborious sounds I couldn't interpret, but I wasn't afraid of her speech anymore. I was used to it and understood you didn't have to grasp it, only be there and accept it. I understood so many things now that had been mysterious. The parade down the dirt roads was to celebrate the dropping of the atom bomb. While people in Hiroshima groped in the ashes for their families, shaved and skinned alive by the heat, the girl who grew to be me marched alongside her mother with her tambourine, banging a spoon against a pot, and dogs took their pleasure. How amazing that that person became me, or that I am she. But I have her eyes. That fire in the oven when Roosevelt died seemed a foretaste of the bigger fire and an echo of fires in bigger ovens, their flames sizzling and sneaking out into our kitchen from the crevices of the broiler door, while inside was the chicken so carefully plucked by the chicken flicker with her clever fingers, her wizardry. I understood that all the times I had watched her, entranced by the primitive and necessary thing she was doing, all the days she flicked chickens hour after hour till her broad lap was a mass of feathers to be emptied into the bin beside her, men in Nevada, also with amazingly skilled and accurate, speedy fingers, also wizards in their fashion, were fingering advanced equipment in order to make a bomb that would save boys like Bobby and bring them home with fanfare. The girl I was saw warriors welcomed back from Korea with a bit less fanfare: that war was undeclared and unclear and inconclusive. She couldn't know that later ones would be received even more grudgingly, without any celebration, left to find their way without the light of torches, because we were never again able to claim innocence. We had television, and we were forced to acknowledge what they had done to return alive, that living flesh had yet again been rendered to ashes. It shook us with doubt, which may be the only kind of progress or education there ever is.

I never minded much the disfigurement of my eye. In the mirror I saw one iris slightly smaller than the other, not very terrible. I couldn't tell when it wandered in its incorrigible, nomadic way; it was others who were made uneasy — I came to detect in people a flicker of discomfort, a glancing away. And my vision was excellent, the "good" eye, in fine fraternal spirit, making up for the defections of its twin. But my parents must have minded, or felt some residual guilt. Early on, they took me to doctors. Big men, as they were called in Brooklyn.

"This one is supposed to be a very big man," my mother would say anxiously to my father, in the front seat of the car.

The trips were long, the big men rarely in Brooklyn. In order to be big, it seemed, you had to be elsewhere, in faraway boroughs, sometimes even New Jersey.

There would be a consultation in a large, hushed, wood-paneled room, where the elderly man, not always big, would do the usual battery of tests, starting off with the simple chart. To my right eye, the chart was a distant porous rectangle with black squiggles skittering over it.

He would ask me once more to cover the good eye. "Do you know your numbers? How many fingers am I holding up?" The fingers were stout and mottled and melted into the vibrating space around them. My mother watched with fevered concentration — puckered lips, glittering eyes — as though to will the correct answer by telepathy; she was feeling vicariously what she took to be my pain at failing the test. She wished to shield me — and by extension, herself — from all of life's pain, and must have felt the pain of failure as among the worst. But I was delighted to fail a test, which I never did at school. I wanted to know failure as I wanted to know everything off limits and out of bounds. I was even fond of the wayward eye that could lead me past the borders and down those broader paths.

One doctor's receptionist suggested, "It might help if you wore your hair a different way, dear. The way you have it sort of calls attention to your eye, don't you think?"

My hair, long, sleek, and very black, hung in bangs like a shade over my forehead. I loved it. It was not like my mother's, not like anyone's hair in Brooklyn. I loved smoothing it down with my hand and feeling its sheen. Squinting my good eye, I disintegrated the plumpness and blondness of the receptionist into a mass of dots writhing on the swivel chair.

How different were these big men of the outlands from the doctors of my fantasies! When I was seven or eight, I put myself to sleep with the same story every night. My skiing accident. I had never skied but I watched skiing every Saturday afternoon at the nearby Carroll Theatre. Movietone News with its dazzling skiers followed the coming attractions and the installment of *Superman* and preceded the movie of the week, which almost always contained scenes of passionate kissing and embracing. And since it was not the custom in Brooklyn to check on the hour of the main feature but simply to saunter in any old time and remain through the next showing, I often had no idea who was kissing whom or why, what the nature of their relation was — whether these were kisses of nascent love and mutual recognition, or illicit kisses, or kisses of recovery after loss or separation, kisses of tragic parting or of reconciliation, or false deceiving kisses, exploitative, opportunistic kisses. Whatever they were mattered less than how beautifully they were executed, the partners performing as if they had been schooled for romance, and I wondered if I would ever learn to do it as well.

But the skiers of Movietone News were always the same, always dazzling, and in bed I would picture myself, in dark glasses, skimming over the gleaming snow and hurling myself out into space till I fell and broke every bone in my body. I was carried to a hospital bed and swathed in splints and bandages. Immobilized, I could only breathe and feel and think. I was fed through straws, thick sugary concoctions like chocolate malteds. A young doctor with dark sweet skin like an Arab or an Indian, tall, who moved with the baleful grace of a giraffe, was brought in especially for my case. He began healing me, working the parts into motion piece by piece. Toes, feet, ankles, knees. Hands, wrists, elbows. Working his way from the extremities inward. Little by little the parts regained sensation and movement. I would test them tentatively, coaxing them out of their torpor. Soon I could sit in a wheelchair. Soon I could walk on crutches. Then with a cane. Finally I took my first hesitant steps unaided. My heart thrilled with gratitude to the doctor who had saved me. He leaned his dark face over me and kissed me on the lips, lightly, with skill, as in the movies. I trembled all over. But that was the beginning of the end. The excitement was greatest when I was half or three-quarters disabled and feeling the parts come to life again under his touch. As soon as I was restored to the full use of my body the thrill evaporated. So, in quest of new excitement, I would go skiing again and have another accident. Even more serious. They feared for my life. Things deep inside were broken this time. Again I was wrapped in bandages, again nothing would move. Again the young doctor, a different one each time, though they all had a family resemblance and all wore white, pristine as the snow I skimmed over. Every night I lay in bed stiff as a plank and slowly felt the parts awaken. Sometimes it took so long for every part to awaken that I fell asleep halfway through.

Other times I couldn't fall asleep at all, no matter how many accidents I suffered, because of the card players downstairs. My father's pinochle men moved from house to house weekly. Every sixth Wednesday my mother set up a bridge table and chairs in the living room and put out bowls of cashew nuts and pretzels and grapes and little round flat chocolates sprinkled with white dots. Big ashtrays, because the men smoked cigars. The cigars came from Havana bearing embossed gold paper rings that my father would give me for my finger and I would pretend I was married. Tall glasses, because the men drank soda. Our soda man, unlike the milkman, came at a reasonable hour and we saw him and spoke to him; he delivered soda in many flavors: cherry, grape, celery, orange, orange-lemon, lemon-grape, cream, root beer, strawberry, cherry-grape, black cherry, black raspberry. My father, a soda addict, would boast to friends, "Audrey doesn't drink any soda," the way a smoker might be proud of a child who had never succumbed, enjoying a mastery of the flesh by proxy. It irked me that he would boast of something not a matter of earned merit but of taste — I just didn't like it. But in Brooklyn, whatever virtues, inherent or acquired, the parents did not possess, it was hoped the children would possess or acquire for them.

The card game men were Mr. Zelevansky, Mr. Tessler,

Mr. Ribowitz, Mr. Singer, and Mr. Capaleggio, whom everyone called Cappy. Only I was expected to call them all Mr., and when for the first time — I was almost sixteen — I addressed Mr. Zelevansky, whom I had known all my life, as Lou, I felt as daring as if I had reached over and unzipped his fly. But that day was far off. Meanwhile when the men arrived one by one and handed their hats and coats to my mother, I was supposed to greet each of them, and when I went up to bed a short while later, say good night. My father was not overly demanding about manners but he had his sticking points: he detested any playing with food at the table, could not bear my referring to my mother as "she," and insisted that I look up at the men's faces and say hello loud and clear. This last I found extremely difficult when I was seven or eight. They were so big and formidable, and there were so many.

"Is it too much to ask," he would grumble to my mother, "to expect her to say hello to people who come to the house?"

This was invariably said in my presence the following day, and instead of answering his question directly my mother defended me. "Yes," I wanted her to say, "it is too much to ask," or even, "No, you have a right to expect that." Either way, whichever she truly thought. It was worse to be defended. She talked about being true to one's self but her instinct was to evade.

Mr. Singer and Mr. Tessler, partners in a furniture business, looked alike, with their jowly cheeks and thick glasses and potbellies, the fourth button of their shirts tugging identically away from the fabric when they leaned back to study their cards. Lanky Mr. Capaleggio, who owned a service station in Queens, wore plaid flannel shirts and had thinning, rust-colored hair and was the only one who smoked a pipe, not cigars. Bald Mr. Ribowitz was tall and skinny with a caved-in chest; I could always remember he had an electrical supplies store, because his head was like a bulb. Mr. Zelevansky and his wife, Belle, were my parents' closest friends. He was an accountant like my father, with thick lips and huge unruly gray eyebrows, and a small bluish scar on one cheek which I liked to think he had gotten in an exciting way, such as a barroom brawl over principles or defending someone from criminal attack, but knowing Brooklyn, I suspected it was probably a household accident.

I knew the men by their voices as well as their looks, and from upstairs in bed could distinguish the soft whine of Mr. Ribowitz, the gentle, phlegmy voice of Mr. Capaleggio, the gruff, conciliating tones of Mr. Zelevansky. The loudest voice was always my father's, bullying, prodding, reproaching, mocking, and I was amazed that the others tolerated him, but they did. For all the years of my childhood.

Pinochle. It didn't sound like English. It sounded inaccessible and dull, like business or taxes, a man's game. I learned to play gin rummy and hearts and canasta and Michigan rummy and poker, but never pinochle, with its cigars and soda and melding, whatever that was. Even the deck was peculiar, truncated, all the cards below the nine banished, as though the low numbers — the ages I was — were too negligible to bother with.

At the end of my skiing fantasies, on those Wednesday nights, I tumbled in and out of troubled sleep with the men's voices in my ears. Melding, Lend-Lease, the Marshall Plan, and Harry Truman, his marriageable daughter, his piano playing. And those words and the images they evoked, war-torn Europe and its starving children, "The Missouri Waltz," lonely Margaret Truman doomed to spinsterhood, as well as the men themselves, paunchy and graying, mingled in my dreams with the skiing and the pain that was not really pain and the young doctors, till I would wake in the dark bewildered: Was I skiing or starving in Europe or home in bed? Was it almost time to line up in the school yard or was there still the whole night to pass?

From time to time there would be a card party. The card players' wives came along and played mah jongg while the men played pinochle, and I had to say hello to twice as many people, though it was not fully twice as agonizing. The women were easier: they were smaller and occupied less space than the men, for one thing, and they occupied their lesser spaces in a less proprietary way, only renting, as it were. They also greeted me in an easier way, as if I were one of them, only smaller still, while the men spoke to me as a member of another species, a house cat, perhaps, with language.

At some point I became aware of a flaw in the fearful symmetry of the card parties. One of the men — I figured out it was sallow Mr. Singer — did not have a wife attached to him. I asked my mother where she was and she brushed me off with one of her vaguenesses. That there might not be a Mrs. Singer didn't occur to me, since unmarried men over thirty were a rarity in Brooklyn, though as a matter of fact there was one right across the street who lived all by himself in a narrow attached row house exactly like ours and was friendly enough, but my mother told me to keep away from him, and later on in junior high there was a French teacher who we girls agreed was unmarried because he was too ugly for any woman to sleep with and moreover smelled bad. Apart from those, the category seemed not to exist, except for widowers. Was Mrs. Singer dead? I asked my mother, and she was vague about that too, though, a bit older now, I pressed her, pointing out there could be no vagueness regarding the question of someone's being dead or alive. She told me to mind my own business and I deduced that if Mrs. Singer were dead it must be of cancer or suicide, the two unmentionable ways to go about dying. I tried to imagine Mr. Singer's grief and loneliness, to bear it in mind when I greeted him, and get a fragrant whiff of drama and tragedy, but it was difficult to work up much emotion when I wasn't sure: my efforts might be wasted. Perhaps she was an invalid, vaporous like the heroine of a Victorian novel or the girl to whom I had brought the class assignments. That would be another kind of drama, more subdued and poignant — but I never heard anyone ask how she was. If she was neither sick nor dead, it was quite possible the Singers were divorced, a situation that seemed to exist only outside Brooklyn, and that would bestow on Mr. Singer an aura of exoticism that, with his potbelly and straining shirt and jowly cheeks, I found him hardly qualified to bear. In any case her absence was convenient and even fortuitous, since the maximum number for a comfortable mah jongg game is five.

On card party nights, in addition to the table in the living room for the men, another was set up in the adjacent dining room for the women. The rooms were connected by a wide arch, and now and then there was banter between the two groups, or perhaps the woman who was East or a man sitting out a hand would wander into the other sector — my father, particularly, liked to graze among the women — but for the most part the evening was spent in separate sectors, like Berlin, which had just been divided up by the Allies, as a punishment, apparently, and to keep Germany impotent and out of harm's way.

In bed I was the unseen audience for a symphony of social noises: the men's table sent up cannonades of belches from the soda consumed, and a crackling of nuts and chips, and the percussive slapping of cards and shuffling of the deck and the voices. Below those sounds was the muted, reedy tinkle of the ivory mah jongg tiles being tossed one by one to the center of the table, then periodically the livelier ensemble of many tiles sliding off the four racks to the center of the table, to be scrambled for the next hand and turned over face down; that was like soft hail on glass, or piano keys struck at random with the soft pedal down. I knew the sound of the tiles well because I helped my mother set up the game before the guests arrived — I would build little walls around each rack, then crash them down to hear the gentle avalanche — and she let me separate the money by color, too, tiny hexagonal plastic wafers in blue and red and green with holes in the middle like doughnuts, and stack them on the little brass poles, attached to each rack, that had joints and could bend in four directions.

The women drank coffee rather than soda — I heard the amiable clink of their cups and saucers — and ate chocolate kisses and sugared fruit candies, orange and cherry and lime, in half-moon shapes with a white line around the arc, and their voices were higher and constant and more convivial: they didn't argue, or if they did it was in small, oblique grace notes, rarely confrontations.

When everyone had played enough, the bridge tables were folded, the extra leaves were put in the dining room table, and the men and women sat down together, husbands next to wives, as my mother brought out coffee and platters of smoked fish and salads. I would join them at the table and listen, friendly, detached, and curious, like an anthropologist, though anthropologists had not been heard of in Brooklyn. And while I enjoyed the food and the talk I secretly vowed that the life I would lead as an adult — as my unknown, not yet existing self; me, that is — far from Brooklyn, in Paris or Cairo, would not include anything resembling card parties. We — my unknown future friends, perhaps at this very moment mired in other Brooklyns but destined to be dark, gaunt, and intense — would not be married. We would sit on the floors of garrets drinking wine, smoking Turkish cigarettes, and talking of art and life. We would be living our lives in the fullest Jamesian sense.

Still later, not in Cairo, merely in Manhattan, after I learned to check on the times of movies so I could begin at the beginning, I also learned it was considered gauche for couples, married or not, to sit together at parties. People should get to know other people. But I knew that wasn't the real reason. A principle was operating in both cases: in the great world, a naughty, mercurial principle of divisiveness, entropy, and unsettling, and in Brooklyn the principle of cohesiveness, a valiant fight against the forces of entropy and division. And these contrary principles mirrored my eyes, the good eye with its seamless smooth coherent world, everything fitting together in just and sensible, enduring relations, and the bad eye breaking things into parts, blurring proportions and distances and harmonies.

The only result of the consultations with the big men was that for a week or two my mother would repeat the exercises in the kitchen as she rolled out dough with her huge wooden rolling pin. I covered my left eye, and she held up fingers dusty with flour.

"Two?"

"Try again."

"Maybe one? Three?"

"You did better in the doctor's office, I think. Are you sure you aren't teasing me?"

"Five?" I was bored. I molded shapes out of leftover dough.

"Come on, Audrey, you can do better."

"Two."

"To thine own self be true," said my mother.

After these spasms of activism the eye was not mentioned. Except for the notes.

Twice a year, at the same moment all over Brooklyn, teachers interrupted their lessons — the division of decimals, the Louisiana Purchase, the relationship between the highwayman and the landlord's black-eyed daughter — to hang eye charts over the map of the world, where our country was always at the center. Twice a year my mother sent a note to have me excused from the test.

I carried it to school like a boulder in my pocket and sat rigid, my cheeks ablaze, until my name was called. I felt the contours of my body cut through the heartless air as I navigated the aisle to the teacher's desk to hand her the note, and I felt the dozens of eyes on my back. Finally I got the idea of giving it to her first thing in the morning. She would read it, offer a doubting glance, and pass over me later when my turn came. Notes from home about health matters were incontrovertible, coming from a higher authority. The hierarchies of authority were complex but everyone grasped them, just as we knew Rock, Paper, Scissors: scissors cuts paper, rock breaks scissors. If we children were paper and the teachers were scissors, home was rock. (Later, only later, paper would cover rock.)

My classmates might look around in surprise — had the teacher made a mistake? — unless they knew me from previous eye tests; one or two bold ones might even question me in a whisper. I whispered back that I didn't have to take the test, I went to a private doctor, echoing my mother's words in the note though they made no sense to me. Who was the private doctor? There were only the anonymous big men we visited, once each. It is perilous to speak someone else's words, above all when you don't understand them. The self vanishes for the moment, leaving you — whatever remains of you, a dumb animal sentience — unbearably weightless and adrift, yearning for your self to return, as a ball swept out by the tide sometimes returns on the next wave.

Twice a year I dreaded the eye test and longed to take it. My eye might well have been a social asset, a conversation piece, like an exotic disease that luckily didn't hurt. But my mother, who had no idea of the classroom's social assets, or of what were my pains and pleasures, wished only to shield me from humiliation. And I was her accomplice: I told her when the tests were scheduled. To do otherwise would have violated her vision of the world, and it was undeniably and irrevocably *her* vision, *her* world, that my good eye saw. In it she spoke with the voice of an oracle and knew which things were proper to enjoy and which caused pain. There were so many times when I longed to make her see what I saw; then we could inhabit the same world, our visions shared and mutually permeating like the atoms of the air. Later on there was one special time . . . But always, the world my bad eye saw was mine alone, invisible to everyone else in Brooklyn, especially to my mother. And I couldn't, back then, place my faith in it. I might choose what to read — the Harvard Classics instead of *Reader's Digest* — and what to dream — the handsome doctor who awakened my battered body. But to trust that solitary vision, to act on my wayward feelings and cherish a different yardstick of pleasure and pain, was hardly possible in that smooth, cohesive place. It would have taken a leap as daring as the leaps of those poor children we read of in the papers every so often, who, after watching *Superman,* trusted the simmering in their bones, spread their wings, and gave themselves to air.

The summer I was fifteen years old — just before my senior year in high school, for I had skipped grades — a new thing under the sun appeared in Brooklyn. Contact lenses. My parents made inquiries. Apparently a lens could be designed that would fit my eye, magnify the iris to the same size as its partner, and discipline its wanderings. The lens would not correct my vision — not possible, the big men said — nor grant me the fabled perception of depth: its use would be purely cosmetic.

Somehow it was decided that I would get this contact lens. I don't recall any solemn sitting down to talk it over. Things would hang mutely in the air and then happen after a while, in Brooklyn; action would be taken, or more often not taken, like Frost's road in the poem I was required to memorize every year, as if no English teacher ever revealed her syllabus to her successor, or else there was a shortage of poems.

> Two roads diverged in a yellow wood,
> And sorry I could not travel both
> And be one traveler, long I stood
> And looked down one as far as I could
> To where it bent in the undergrowth; . . .
>
> I took the one less traveled by,
> And that has made all the difference.

But since my father expounded on politics while watching television and grumbling about the Senate investigations, I knew about logrolling. I wanted to take an acting class at a community center at the closest edge of Manhattan, just over the Williamsburg Bridge — a girl at school already making tentative outbound forays had enticed me.

"Acting?" said my mother. She had had theatrical leanings, too, before settling into marriage. "Since when are you interested in acting?"

"I don't know. Does it matter?" We were on the back porch, hanging clothes on the line. I handed her each wet thing from the basket and she clipped it to the rope with wooden clothespins like tiny claws, every T-shirt and sock neatly attached to its companions, all holding hands the way we had been forced to do on line in the school yard. After clipping each item she moved the rope smartly along the pulley. She was so adept at using the pulley, so economically clever in the apportioning of rope, that she could fill almost the whole line, top and bottom layers, a feat in mechanical physics I now and then tried to re-envision — long after, when she was dead and I tossed damp laundry into the maw of a gas dryer — but never successfully.

"No, it doesn't matter. Just that until a few years ago you could barely talk to strangers, so how are you going to get up and emote in front of an audience?" Squeak, went the line, another few feet of rope became free, and she grabbed a wet pyjama top from my hands.

What she said was Brooklyn logic, yet it was entirely clear to me that those things were unconnected. Or if they were, if they had to be, I sensed that my infantile shyness might well contribute to my success as an actress. This was not something that could be explained in our language, so I thrust a handful of wet socks at her.

"Don't you see, if I have my eye fixed I'll be a perfect specimen and then I can go on the stage."

"Very funny. You'll be a comedian."

"Come on, it's only four dollars a week."

Maybe she thought I could fulfill her discarded dreams, maybe she was thankful I had been docile about the contact lens. She agreed. But I made her nervous. She dropped a nightgown and I had to climb over the porch railing and into the Schneiders' tiny back yard to retrieve it.

The road the contact lens represented was more traveled by. Conscientious parents pursued standardization as Calvinists performed good works, doing what they could for salvation regardless of the unfathomable caprices of destiny. They processed their daughters like ore or sugar, to refine and, in the refining, transform. Wealthier girls were given elocution lessons, to leach the remnants of East European inflections from their tongues. In our more modest neighborhood, orthodontists lined the roofs of pliant mouths with grotesque plastic bite plates. The girls wearing bite plates always made me think of the passage in one of my favorite childhood books, where Black Beauty has the dread bit inserted, in preparation for a life of submissive toil:

> Those who have never had a bit in their mouths, cannot think how bad it feels; a great piece of cold hard steel as thick as a man's finger to be pushed into one's mouth, between one's teeth and over one's tongue, with the ends coming out at the corner of your mouth, and held fast there by straps over your head, under your throat, round your nose, and under your chin; so that no way in the world can you get rid of the nasty hard thing; it is very bad! yes, very bad! at least I thought so; but I knew my mother always wore one when she went out, and all horses did when they were grown up; and so, what with the nice oats, and what with my master's pats, kind words, and gentle ways, I got to wear my bit and bridle.

One of the Barbaras had her nose "fixed." I visited her in the hospital where she lay covered by a coarse white sheet, mustardy rings around her eyes, which shone nonetheless with relief that the thing was done and with hope for a better life as a result.

"The doctor broke her nose with a hammer," I told my mother. I pictured the doctor swinging his hammer at Barbara's anesthetized body the way a woodcutter swings his axe at a tree.

"Oh, go on! What are you telling me?"

"He did. She said so."

"A hammer? I don't believe it."

"Don't, then."

"To thine own self be true," my mother murmured, lowering a raw, superbly plucked chicken into a pot of water.

"I am."

"No kidding?" She frowned. "Who knows, maybe it's worth it in the long run. Be glad you don't have to go through that. Your nose is perfect."

It was done "for their own good," so that eventually the girls could become "settled." In effect, resettled after the brief uproariousness of childhood. Screaming, resisting, the infant emerges from the profound settledness of the enveloping womb into the unsettledness of the universe. The mother's task was to guide it back as quickly as possible to a womblike state, there to remain until the ultimate settledness of death.

Settled. Even the word, the popping, damp *tl* followed by that thudding *d,* sounded like a lowering, a surrender. My bad eye saw the gravelly residue of a grand experiment, all blaze and color and metamorphosis, sinking heavily to the bottom of the test tube, sadly exiled from the action above. I had seen such things happen in test tubes in the chemistry lab, though not, alas, in my own — I could not call spirits from the briny deep, maybe because during the first two weeks of chemistry I myself had been exiled to the far end of the lab, which the teacher called Siberia. My crime was touching the equipment — test tubes and Bunsen burner — before being given official permission to do so.

"Settled" meant following the prescribed plan for your life, becoming a person whose every impulse would pass an inspection as rigorous as Mrs. Bluestone's; an impeccable person with no reservations or questions, capable of nothing questionable either, merely of lying inert at the bottom of the test tube while the experiments continued elsewhere.

"They can't seem to settle," my mother would say of the recklessly unmarried older daughters of neighbors. For that was the most obvious meaning of "settled" — if not getting married, at least training one's mind towards marriage. School cooperated, offering the Pre-Marriage course — for seniors only, a reward, as marriage itself would be the promised end — taught by Mrs. Carlino, a twice-divorced woman, rumor tittered. Twice divorced and currently married meant she must have slept with three different men in her life, which was scandalously in excess of Brooklyn requirements as well as inconvenient: my mother maintained that when divorced people remarried, the ex-partner was a presence in the bed like a ghost or a shadow. Mrs. Carlino's mimeographed sheets circulated through school like *samizdat* writings, and it was these notorious mimeographed sheets, more than any universal instinct for marriage, that made her course so popular. I was taking it, just for the exposure; aside from Mrs. Carlino I didn't know anyone who had been divorced even once (unless mysterious sallow Mr. Singer). The most famous sheet, and the most difficult to obtain without actually enrolling, was on Dating and Courtship: Mrs. Carlino allegedly gave the definitive meanings of Necking and Petting — to her students, the climax of the term's work. But so far, one week into the term, we had covered only menstrual cramps. They were imaginary, Mrs. Carlino informed us as she demonstrated, from her crouch on the floor, an exercise to relieve them.

"She seems like a settled type," my mother remarked about a few friends I brought home, one of the Susans in particular. Susan answered questions willingly, carried her empty milk glass to the sink, and smiled a lot. When I drilled her in French verbs she insisted on pronouncing the silent *ent* of the third-person plural present tense; if she didn't, she claimed, she would forget it was there. Her placid glistening teeth, her obedient hair, her muscleless body, fit unquestioningly into space. She had the slowest walk in Brooklyn — there was nowhere she had to go with any urgency; her French pronunciation didn't matter, for surely she would never get as far as Paris. She drifted through the unresisting air, which shaped itself around her like a silky cocoon.

So powerful was placid Susan and all she stood for that, with my mother's encouragement, she persuaded me to pledge for one of the illegal, secret sororities that flourished at school. Girls pledged not to enjoy the advantages of membership but to see if they would be accepted. Then they could judge others in turn, by standards teasingly obscure: a Kafka story, a Calvinist's heaven.

That I agreed to pledge is hard for me to believe: it does not fit with the girl I think I was, or the girl I am attempting to reconstitute in the telling, who is perhaps turning out to be not the girl I really was. I am confused about who I was: why else would I need to tell this story of my eye? The confusion is that I seem to have grown up into someone who could not have been me as a child. Yet in the telling the girl grows to sound more and more like the woman I became. The voice overcomes her. The real girl with her layers concealing me becomes more elusive the more I tell. She has been superseded, but I am sure she existed. As I try to find her in me, I keep finding me in her.

I must have pledged for the drama of it, for I was almost bound to be rejected. I can reconstruct, if not quite remember, how I felt: yes, even the misery of rejection would be more welcome to her than stale corridors and gym suits and teachers. It would be something she could feel, and a kind of knowledge beneath the surface, too. For misery drew me then, as more complex and instructive than settledness, or even happiness. Pledging for the sorority would also ease my mother's doubts about the acting class. I am sure I — the girl — would have thought of that.

Above all, settled meant "settling for," as in making the best of a bad bargain, such as one's life, or as my parents had settled without question for the damaged goods brought to them from the hospital nursery. That settledness, that passivity in the face of circumstance, led me to the office of the contact lens doctor.

⌐⌐

An even greater postwar novelty than contact lenses was television, that most powerful lens. People regarded it as dwarf movies, and it was viewed in the dark. We were among the last on our block to succumb, and our living room took on a perpetual gloom, a cloak of grief. Farewell to light. We lived — all of Brooklyn did — like cave families who sat around sighing in the dark until the accidental discovery of fire.

From the flickering eye of the room beamed the image of the man my father called "the pig," in fuzzy black and white on the evening news, marbly eyes darting, shoulders hunching, spit gathering at the corners of his mouth, while my father, stretched out on the red couch, ground his teeth audibly, gnawed on his cigar, and said, "Somebody's going to get that bastard one of these days."

This was Joseph McCarthy, the senator, and he did resemble a pig, with his balloony face and small mean eyes and snout. He moved like the larger sort of pig or ox, too, a boar or buffalo, rolling his cylinder of a body about in one unarticulated chunk, great shudders rippling down from his shoulders. Savagery had frozen on his face, vindicating my mother's warnings. When he confronted his prey his lips glistened with the foam of condensed rage and his cheeks and eyes exuded a brutish ardor, like pigs' faces when they make ready to fall on the orts and peels heaped in their trough.

"But what is he doing?" I asked when it began. I was in junior high and had been warned that chaos leads to communism.

"Oh, he just wants power. Power mad. It's not even communism. Ego."

This was confusing. It had to be communism; that was all everyone talked about, especially Miss Kuznetzov in History class.

During a commercial, my father explained that power was the ability to use and exploit and even destroy other people for your own purposes, you merely had to find a timely pretext, and while unfortunately that was what the world was all about, power and greed, in this case it happened to be unconstitutional. It was precisely for madmen such as this one that we had a constitution. Law was a curb on passion. Without it where would we be. And so forth.

It was the first time I had heard anyone openly suggest the world spun on an axis of passion, with power and greed its poles. The living room darkened. I closed my good eye and it grew darker still, splintering into implications. Was there no real goodness, then, in human nature? Was all our civilized behavior contrived, induced by artificial constraints? If left to our true desires, would we be savages? All the secrets I felt and hid began to throb: what might I find myself doing if these secrets demanded freedom and expression? How could my father have uttered such thoughts in our own living room, where the very walls, listening and fathoming, might collapse in rebellion — what law decreed they must stand forever and shield us?

Worse, these notions were not entirely unfamiliar — they had the trembling, shadowy echo of things deeply known, the kind of knowledge Socrates claimed is inborn and waits, dormant, to be fired into life by the bellows of inquiry; or the kind of knowledge Wordsworth says we forget from infancy as shades of the prison house begin to close, though these shivery recollections of mine were hardly the billowy glories of the infinite that trailed Wordsworth's cherubs.

But in Brooklyn! It was everything Brooklyn kept at bay, the very reason for Brooklyn's existence.

My mother entered from the kitchen and sat down to watch. My father was grumbling at the screen again.

"What is it?" she said. "Oh, him again."

She couldn't know, I decided. She was Brooklyn's spokesman. Through her, Brooklyn said we must be good because it was good to be good, we were made to be good and would be happiest being good, we must only stop doing what we liked and listen instead to our elders, who knew what good was.

"Why don't they just throw him out, then, if it's unconstitutional?" I asked.

"They will, they will." My father grunted. "It'll just take some time."

"But I don't get it. Why do people sit there and answer?"

"Because they're afraid. Their jobs, their families. And they have good reason to be. Power is real. People are being destroyed right and left."

"Why do *we* just sit here, then? Why don't we get up and do something?"

"Do what?"

"I don't know. Sign a petition. Write to your congressman. Make a public statement."

"A public statement." My father gave his characteristic sound — a sneering laugh, or laughing sneer — and relit his cigar. "A public statement. You go out and make a public statement and see what happens."

My mother groaned. "Oh, don't tell her such things."

I often puzzled over how much she knew, or cared, about the world outside Brooklyn. She had certain icons she revered and praised when their names came up — primarily the Roosevelts, Eleanor as well as Franklin — but her reverence seemed inspired more by their characters than their politics, or, rather, she saw no possible distinction between the two. Otherwise her feelings were engaged when the evening news concerned personal disasters, when miners were trapped and their wives waited wretchedly at the entrance to the mine, or a prominent businessman was proven to be a racketeer and his innocent family wept, or an entire household was murdered in its sleep by a motiveless lunatic. Then she clicked her tongue and shook her head and wondered aloud at what was happening to the world, and at how human nature and moral fiber had eroded since her youth, when people had character and fed hungry strangers at the gate and you could leave your door unlocked at any hour.

"If you tell her things like that," she pursued, "next thing you know, she'll go out and do it."

"Well, why not?" I said. "This is supposed to be a democracy. And you all sit here like sheep. What if it was one of your friends?"

"It wouldn't be one of our friends," she said. "We don't know people like that."

"I wish we did," I retorted. She was right. There was no one worth accusing in this dead backwater, no artists, no communists, no adventurers, no one with a soul. No drama or upheaval could happen here where we languished on the periphery, in the shadows of the world. Even McCarthy was only a fat face on a flat screen, no danger. My body ached with boredom as potent as a drug injected into my veins.

"*Schmuck,*" my father taunted the television screen. "Communists! Communists! You wouldn't know a communist if he came and sat on your goddamn head."

I remembered the communists in *The Saturday Evening Post* illustration, rhythmically pounding their sticks on the bucket covering the victim's head. McCarthy was pounding. And my father, if he had the power, would pound in return. Did the captured American in the story talk? Would I?

"Communism," my father shouted at the screen, "is a system of economic organization of goods and services! Communism is not a moral flaw!"

"Shush, for God's sakes!" warned my mother. "The walls

are thin. They can hear you on East New York Avenue."

"Who!" He turned on her, ready to pounce. "Who'll hear me? Rosenbloom? Schneider?" Our next-door neighbors. "They're illiterate anyway. Let them hear!"

"I give up." She rose and started for the kitchen. "For me it's enough to live a decent life. I can't take the problems of the world on my shoulders."

"So who asked you to?" he hurled after her.

McCarthy disappeared, replaced by a commercial for Camel cigarettes. My father's eyes gazed sullenly at the screen.

"It's very easy," I remarked, "to yell at a television set."

"Oh, so you would do better, I suppose. The whole country is shaking with fear, the President doesn't know what to do with him, and you would do better."

"I wouldn't answer those questions, anyway. I'd tell him to go to hell. I wish I were up there."

I did. I yearned to be older, and so prominent in some field or other — acting or politics or journalism — that I was worthy of suspicion. McCarthy would accuse me and I would crush him by my intrepid performance. How dare you? I would answer with passion but dignity. How dare you ask me these insolent questions? My beliefs and my sympathies are my private affair, guaranteed by the Constitution. No one tells me how to think! The audacity! You have exceeded the boundaries of civil behavior. Moreover you're nothing but a pig. Nothing but a pack of cards . . . I would fix him with the eye that saw the thing behind the thing, the essence behind the surface image, and since he was nothing but an image he would disappear, melting into his surroundings. This was what I was made for, this was my mission, not the life of a schoolgirl in Brooklyn.

"Well," said my father, "who knows? Maybe you would. I hope you would."

I was so accustomed to his sarcasm, I could so mechanically invert much of what he said, like a simultaneous translator, that I hardly grasped when he was in earnest. We exchanged a brief embarrassed look. "Audrey dear, do me a favor, will you? Go upstairs and bring me two Alka-Seltzers and a glass of water."

McCarthy's was not the only crusade. As secret as his was flagrant was the crusade of Miss Schechter, the Geometry teacher. Miss Schechter held the passionate conviction that it was wrong and immodest for girls of thirteen to wear bras before, in her judgment, they were necessary. Padded bras and the ultimate, falsies, abetted this practice and must be extirpated wherever they were found. Her Savonarola eyes scanned the rows of seats, scrutinizing bosoms — it was an era of tight chartreuse and fuchsia sweaters — and lit on a daily suspect. Leaving the class with a difficult proof to work on, Miss Schechter marched the girl to the girls' room.

Children get used to things. At first there was pity for the victim, her trembling and pallor, our whispers and blushes; halfway through the term it was part of the geometrical routine, and even the boys lost interest and simply welcomed the break. Pride played its part too. No one could actively wish to be chosen, yet who could wish to be totally overlooked? What did she do in the girls' room? What did she really want? I asked one of the Judys, a giggler and gossiper who had been picked several times. "She looks," said Judy laconically. It must be beyond gossip.

I would never know. I was safe, braless. The crucial lesson of Joseph McCarthy was lost on me. What a surprise to hear my name called.

"But I'm not wearing a bra," I murmured as I trailed down the corridor after Miss Schechter, striding along full of purpose.

"We'll see about that!"

She opened the door and stepped aside so I could precede her. It was during class — no one else was there. We passed the three stalls and stopped near the frosted window. I backed off and leaned against the sink.

"All right, let's see."

I stared at her.

"Raise your sweater."

I must have heard wrong. If I raised my sweater she would accuse me of a ghastly *faux pas*. With pursed lips, she gave a tiny jerk of her head upwards, and I had to allow what I had heard.

I did it. It wouldn't have occurred to me to refuse. I could defy McCarthy because he operated under well-known laws, but Miss Schechter was a teacher.

It is another of those acts I have trouble, now, believing I did; I wish I were making it up or reporting from hearsay, appropriating the scene to make the narrative more telling. Perhaps I am, I hope I am. Once again, the line blurs between what happened and what I recall as happening.

Impossibly, I raised my pink sweater to my collarbone and Miss Schechter, hands behind her back as if locked there by force of will, studied my incipient breasts. I felt the humiliation less than the stratospheric chill of impossibility. This was Brooklyn. School. I was a dreamer with a dream life. Despite what people think, dreamers are very clear about what is fantasy and what is reality — they have to be.

I had nowhere to look so I looked at her face. Grim as always, frozen in grimness, it was an olive-skinned face with premature papery wrinkles stitching the parts together, nose carefully stitched to the cheeks, eyes carefully stitched into their sockets . . . The mouth was thin and grooved, like a cord. The chin quivered. I moved my eyes lower. She wore a nondescript brown outfit, a sweater and cardigan set. Her breasts, which I had never noticed before, were flat scallops of dough slapped onto her chest. I looked up again. Her black eyes gave off light.

"All right," she said finally. "Pull it down now, what are you waiting for!"

"I told you," I couldn't resist saying, since I was good in Geometry.

"I misjudged." The stitches of her face loosened. "I should

have known you were a decent girl, Audrey. But why are you squinting? Is something wrong with your eyes? Maybe you need glasses."

Does it seem shocking that no parents were told, that we protected them as we protected Miss Schechter? It simply wasn't in the language. Besides, I thought my parents would no more question a teacher's authority than a doctor's. But I too misjudged. Sexual misconduct would have broken authority, in Brooklyn, as surely as scissors cut paper and rock breaks scissors.

Miss Schechter gazed at my breasts as though they were the first on earth, a mutation, the way she might gaze through a microscope at a brand-new virus had she been a scientist, or upon an illuminating figure drawn on the sands of the Mediterranean had she been Euclid. ("Euclid alone has looked on beauty bare," motherly Mrs. Gompers, the English teacher, recited to us in the afternoons, and everyone in Miss Schechter's morning class erupted in giggles, to be chided for immaturity — "I certainly wouldn't expect this from ninth-graders.") Miss Schechter's gaze made breasts and all their connotations arcane and rare, not ubiquitous: family heirlooms taken out of their locked case only on very special occasions.

Her gaze reflecting the rarity of breasts haunts me to this day. When I walk along a European beach where the women lie with bare breasts like dozens of pairs of huge eyes in every shape and shade staring blank and quivering at the sun, I shudder and want to look away; like a prudish lustful child I want to cover them, toss an enormous blanket as I would over beautiful obscenities that can consume the retina. Oh, it's only a passing shudder. I do it myself when I'm there, take off the top of the bathing suit — after all, if there's anything I know how to do it's how to conform. I never knew anything but doubleness; I never had the cozy expectation that what I feel and what I do should converge.

Despite our silence, Miss Schechter's passion saturated the

air like humidity, sliding into our pores. The next term in First Aid, the ninth-grade girls spent six giddy weeks bandaging one another — splints, slings, tourniquets, knee bandages, head bandages — all at once grasping the tactile reality of bodies, the thickness of arms and the bony resistance of knees, the delicate trellis of the ribs, the damp of the inner elbow, and the tepid smell of skin and hair. We fell on one another in springtime hysteria, giggly and wild and drunk with the chance to touch and to know. Not a day passed without some girl murmuring, "Schechter would love this, wouldn't she?"

It was close to ten-thirty as I started down the hall to my parents' bedroom. I had to arrange to meet my mother the following day, for she was determined to accompany me to the contact lens doctor's and had been anticipating the trip to Manhattan as though it were Constantinople. Their room was dark, or nearly dark, the door closed. I paused. When I was small I used to barge in without warning, but now I was aware that they might be doing the things described in the book with the thick wine-colored cover, which I found under a pile of magazines in their bedroom when I was nine.

For months I had kept the book beneath school papers in a night table drawer and would read it in bed — a kind of dessert after the Harvard Classics or the Little Leather Library — until I knew the best parts by heart. Then I put it back under the magazines, gone but not forgotten. A kindly, pedagogic book, it treated its subject as a procedure — unusual almost to the point of requiring apology — that could not be executed properly without instructions, like how to curtsey in the presence of the Queen of England, or what to do in a Tibetan religious rite; and also infinitely delicate and complex, like repairing the engine of a truck or performing brain surgery. It was a manual for first-timers: it called the man "the husband" and the woman "his bride." His bride was a tender, timid creature who needed to be handled with the utmost care and solicitude. It was hard to gauge from the book whether his bride knew what her role was, or whether she had any functioning consciousness at all, since the text was addressed to the husband. His bride was a soft pet, something feathered and fluttery you could turn round in your hands, a bird that had lost all urge to fly.

The husband was supposed to begin by kissing his bride gently, stroking her body and her breasts, and then carefully enter her, lying on top. This was the ideal. But in many if not most cases, the kindly instructor acknowledged — with a tolerance familiar to me from my mother's tolerance of the chicken flicker's cleft palate and the tolerance we were taught to feel towards people of other races — the bride might not be "ready." In that event the husband was to take his bride on his lap, first removing or at least raising her nightgown, wet his fingers in his mouth, and gently spread the saliva over her genital area. I thought of my mother's cold cream and my father's shaving cream, which I had seen them spread on their faces with three fingers. After a bit of this, the husband replenishing the saliva from time to time, they could lie down again.

Now came the moment for his bride's single initiative: when "ready," she was supposed to tell him to "come up over." My body jerked with an electric shock when I first read those words, and every time after, too, I shuddered and winced as I felt them approaching on the page. Through my unwilling eyes the words suffused me with shame; what mortified me was not the invitation itself but the unnatural coupling of objectless prepositions, the vast and ominous clumsiness of the phrase. It seemed even more keenly peculiar under the circumstances, since no other words were apparently spoken.

"Come on over," which sounded almost the same, and so amiable and smooth, was a way of inviting someone to your house. But "up over"? I recalled the dogs on the field at twilight years ago, when our gamboling parade celebrated the bomb that ended the war. The black dog really was "up over." But people in such positions? The words suggested very different sorts of activities: mountain climbing, or scaling fire escapes and roofs, as I did in the apartment building of friends around the corner on Montgomery Street. Or Red Rover, which we played in the streets on summer evenings, when the light lasted forever and the parents sat out on the porches reading newspapers and eating cherries and watermelon. One child got down on all fours and the others leaped over her in turn. "Red Rover, Red Rover, let Audrey come over." I would put my hands on the back of the crouching girl or boy, straddle, and leapfrog over.

And "come up over" what? Over the bride herself. She was referring to herself, her body, but not naming herself — no pronoun to satisfyingly close the scaling prepositions. The words were maddening, itching with incompleteness and balked expectations. I would have to do those things someday, and though they seemed alien and absurd — especially having someone's spit all over me — I didn't worry about it, I assumed I would grow into it like everyone else. But those words? I could never, never speak them. It pained me to think the skilled and graceful heroines in the movies spoke them after they were married. Maybe the book was wrong. That might not be the only way to go about it, or even the correct way. My father was always telling my mother not to believe everything she read.

In any event, I was older now. I knew enough not to barge through a closed door. I took another step down the hall and saw that in fact the door was open a few inches. There was a faint light I recognized as the flicker from the television screen. I had badgered my parents so much about the gloom — playing on their conformities, quoting *The Ladies' Home Journal* and its six sister magazines on the subject of the home as an open, cheerful place to which a child should be proud to invite her friends — that they had moved the TV upstairs to their bedroom, restoring light to the living room.

Edging closer, I heard low canned voices, one of which I knew well. Safe. They were watching "Break the Bank."

"Are you up?" I said, and nudged the door open a few more inches. My parents' heads turned from the TV set to me, parallel forty-five-degree angles. They were sitting side by side, my father in his striped pyjamas and my mother in a scoop-necked sleeveless nylon nightgown. Very neat and chaste, with the covers drawn up to their chests. One of my father's hands was invisible; something moving under the covers, clearly his missing hand, stopped abruptly.

"If you insist on going with me," I said to my mother, "we'd better arrange where to meet after school."

"What do you mean, if I insist? You're my child. I have to see what this doctor proposes to do to you."

"Okay! So where do you want to —"

"Quiet!" exclaimed my father, raising his free hand as if to stave off an aggressor. "Hold it a minute, will you? He's almost ready to break the bank."

I entered and condescended to look at the screen. The category was biblical figures. I sat down on the edge of the bed. Bert Parks asked a moon-faced man with a bow tie the name of Samson's father, and the man answered promptly and correctly. Manoah. Clamorous applause and clanging of bells, lights flashing.

"Amazing," said my mother. "Amazing, the intelligence of some people."

My father nodded his head several times, tightening his lips, grudgingly impressed. He lit a cigar, tossing away the gold ring he used to give to me.

One more correct answer and the round man would break the bank, winning one hundred twenty-eight thousand dollars.

"I knew that too," I said.

"Really? So what are you doing sitting here?" my father snapped. "Go on TV, make yourself useful."

"I did know," I protested.

"Okay, okay. I didn't mean any harm. Quiet."

The TV camera panned the audience. The faces were glazed with suspense, the bodies leaning forward as one stiff, excited body.

"To break the bank, can you tell me," said Bert Parks, "what biblical warrior promised God to sacrifice the first of his possessions that he saw, if he could return home from battle victorious, and ended up sacrificing his own daughter?"

Silence. The contestant clasped his hands and rolled his big eyes heavenward, his Adam's apple jiggling above the bow tie. Bert Parks inclined his body helpfully towards him. My father puffed on his cigar. My mother's lips parted.

"Five seconds," said Bert Parks.

"Jephthah," I said.

My mother tilted her head towards me with a trace of apprehension. "What did you say?"

"Jephthah," I enunciated clearly.

A long buzz sounded and the studio audience groaned in unison.

"Sorry," said Bert Parks, "the correct answer is Jephthah."

I shrugged.

"How do you like that? She broke the bank," said my mother. She kept staring at me, as though she had created a monster. "Did you hear that?" She prodded my father.

"Very smart, Audrey. Very smart. Jephthah, eh?"

"Uh-huh." A commercial for spark plugs was coming on. The spark plugs were dancing to a tune everyone in Brooklyn knew.

Finally he grinned. "You really broke the bank," he conceded. "Goddamn! Not bad, Audrey, not bad. Jephthah. Ha! So what else do you know?"

"He didn't intend to sacrifice her. He promised the first thing he saw as he got near his house. He must have figured it would be a cow or a sheep or something, but it turned out his daughter was running down the road to congratulate him.

So, you know what God is like, he had to keep his promise."

"How do you like that?" mused my mother. "You could have won over a hundred and twenty thousand dollars."

"How'd you get so smart?" asked my father.

"I read. I don't watch quiz shows."

"Smart aleck. Maybe you don't even need to go to college, you know so much already."

This was our way of raising important issues. The issue of college would be a touchy one, I knew. They assumed I would go to Brooklyn College as other girls in the neighborhood did; they knew nothing yet of my dreams of the Sorbonne, or at least of somewhere outside Brooklyn.

"His mother was a harlot, actually," I added. "Jephthah's."

"What has that got to do with it?" asked my mother.

"I don't know. Nothing, maybe. Just a fact."

"So what was the daughter's name," asked my father, "if you know so much?"

Audrey, I wanted to snap back, thinking of the contact lens appointment tomorrow, and all the times, when I was small and shy, that he had forced me to say hello to his card players. But it might sound a trifle hyperbolic. "She didn't have a name, as far as I know. I mean, she didn't really need one, did she? She just had to put her head on the block."

"I was under the impression that Jews just sacrificed cattle," said my mother.

"That's true. This was an exception. Oh, she was also a virgin."

"Well, she wasn't married, she was still living in her father's house. I should hope so."

"We wouldn't want her following in her grandmother's footsteps." My father relit the cigar that had gone dead in the ashtray.

"But she felt bad about that."

"I can certainly understand that," said my mother.

A new contestant was introduced, a slender young man

with glasses and greasy hair, who chose the category of Sports Figures.

"The Greeks have a general sacrificing his daughter to win a battle too," I continued. "Or, specifically, to make the wind blow so his ships can sail."

"I really don't care for all this talk about sacrificing children." My mother had had three miscarriages and, finally, me. She believed, or professed, that children were sacred. She and my father were so grateful when I was born, and healthy too, she had told me. So grateful that they forgot to mention the eye injury in the hospital. What was a little smudge after three losses?

"Max Schmeling!" declared my father. This was in answer to a Sports Figures question: What German boxer did Joe Louis defeat in 1938 to keep his world heavyweight championship title? My father won twelve thousand dollars.

"Oh, I remember that fight. We heard it on the radio with Lou and Belle. It was before you were born, Audrey. I must have been almost pregnant, though."

"It was a great fight," said my father, "because in 1938 everyone wanted to see him knock out a Kraut, and he did. He finished him off in the first round. Quiet. Here's another."

The next question concerned football, in which none of us had any interest, so I said, "The difference between the Greek general and the Jewish one is that the Greek sacrificed her in order to get started, but Jephthah did it afterwards. I mean, the battle was already won, so . . . Doesn't that seem a little bit, you know, too much?"

"You said yourself, he had to keep his word," replied my father.

"Maybe he could have broken his word and sacrificed himself."

"That's not the point. He was acting for a whole nation. He had to overlook personal considerations. That's what men do in time of war."

"Yeah, what does anyone's private suffering matter in the long run, right? You can probably even get to enjoy it if you practice enough."

My father pointed the glowing cigar at me. "What are you implying, Audrey? That Jews like to suffer? You know what kind of people say that? Do you know what that kind of attitude can lead to? I'm surprised at you."

Good. I loved to surprise them. They needed to be surprised.

"I don't think it has anything to do with Jews. I think it's a shame either way. Before, after," said my mother. "I don't see any difference. A child is a child in any religion."

"Actually Jephthah's daughter wasn't the only exception," I said. "Look at Abraham and Isaac. I mean, what kind of God could expect that? That surprises me. It really does. It goes against everything he himself taught. Be fruitful and multiply? Thou shalt not kill? Did he forget? Frankly, I always thought Abraham would have been a better person if he refused. I mean, God has lower moral standards than the people he created."

"It was only a test. It didn't happen in the end, remember."

"Oh, sure, at the last minute. Big deal. He made his point, though. And what if it had been a minute later?" I was standing up and pacing around the room, gesticulating as my father did when he got excited. "But as a test of character I would say, in my opinion, Abraham failed. Some parent. I mean, that's some example he sets. It doesn't exactly inspire the younger generation with trust, does it? Not to mention faith in God. Oh sure, I should believe in someone who would tell my parents to sacrifice me so easily, just to see if they were really obedient. Did anyone ever think of how Isaac felt? Wasn't he a person too? Or just a thing to play around with to prove something?"

"Look here, I don't appreciate it any more than you do," said my father. "But I don't want to hear you criticizing your own people. There are enough of the others who criticize us. You don't understand the first thing about all this. Wars have been fought because people spread wrong ideas. Now move out of the way. I can't see the screen."

"Audrey." My mother gave me her shrewd, to-thine-own-self-be-true look. "What are you carrying on for? It's just a contact lens. You know it's for your own good."

I sighed. Bert Parks and the greasy young man were back. The question was about hockey. I went to the door. "How about if I meet you at the Utica Avenue subway at three-thirty? At the change booth."

"Okay, three-thirty. Wear something nice. We'll be in the city."

The dreaded day arrived. With my mother, I ventured on the subway from Brooklyn to Park Avenue in mythic Manhattan, a mere river away, though it felt like another planet as we emerged into brilliant light. Park Avenue with its sleek buildings and uniformed doormen was awash in sunlit glamour — it was a warm September and the kind of day when each grain of mica in the sidewalk gleams. I was stepping on the jeweled pavements that had brought my grandparents here in the first place. Everyone on the street was slim and fair and brushed to perfection. Everyone was of a higher order of being, including the doormen. I had the absurd feeling I might not understand the language spoken here. The cars were faster and larger and shinier. The traffic lights twinkled brighter. Even the sky seemed a better blue, an impossibly sophisticated blue.

We passed a magnificent old church, reddish nubby stone, warm, grand contours. I had never seen anything like it in Brooklyn, even though Brooklyn was called the City of Churches — puzzlingly, since nearly everyone I knew there was Jewish. I wanted to stop and look but my mother hurried me along, saying we mustn't be late. I knew she wouldn't stop on the way back either. She could not be true to herself and admire a church.

— 62 —

The doctor's waiting room was like others I had waited in, with inexpressive leather chairs and ceramic ashtrays and prints of snow-covered cottages on the walls. He went in for glossy fashion magazines, along with the usual *Life*s and *Look*s, as well as a few *Junior Scholastic*s for his young patients. "He won't be long," said the middle-aged receptionist encouragingly, and very soon a door opened and we were beckoned into the office.

The doctor, reputedly a pioneer in lenses, was a tall fair-skinned man with thinning hair, a sandy mustache, and glasses — I noticed at once he had not availed himself of the new technology. He didn't seem nearly as ancient as the doctors we had seen in my childhood, but then again I was older now. He wore a white shirt and tie, without a jacket or white coat, and there was a controlled energy in the way he moved. Unlike the spacious, genteel offices of earlier big men, his examining room, where my mother perched on the edge of a brown leather couch, was small, draped, and cluttered, dominated by a huge leather chair. There I sat facing an array of equipment like the space flight paraphernalia in science fiction movies. He was a man of few words, polite though aloof, as if distracted by higher matters. He ran through the usual tests, patterns projected onto a screen, illusions of height and width, hidden diagrams, all the ingenious eye doctor games that had once amused but now bored me. His face bent close to mine as he examined my eye; his breath smelled of something unfamiliar, heady and sweet but sharp. With machines pressed against my eye, he took measurements and wrote them down and said good-bye.

A week later we returned and he presented the lens in a little snap-open case, the kind in which suitors present engagement rings.

Primitive contact lenses were not the minuscule glistening transparencies they are today. Mine was a hard, clear plastic disk with about the diameter of a half dollar and the thickness of a fine china cup. It was molded like a human eye, a raised circle in the center for the iris. The lens suggested a squashed miniature volcano, or the bowl of a specially designed spoon for a rare fruit. It would cover the entire visible portion of the eye, white and all, like half an eggshell.

The doctor squirted some liquid on both sides of the thing and, in the swift sneaky manner of doctors, spread my upper and lower lids with his fingers and slipped it in. I wanted to howl in protest. Feelings in the body rarely correspond to what causes them, the nervous system being so desperately inventive. A burn can feel as if the skin is stretched and split on a rack, a cramp in the gut feels like an iron lasso. But this sensation, perhaps because I had seen the lens first, was entirely accurate. I felt as if I had a hard plastic disk the size of a half dollar trapped between my lids, and I marveled that my mother showed no urge to shield me from the pain, as she did from so many insignificant ones.

He leaned over me, peering into my armored eye, his liquory breath dazing me and making me slightly sick, his right leg brushing against mine, producing an ellipse of warmth. I saw the pores of his cheeks, the dark of his nostrils; his gray pupils, enormous behind the thick glasses, seemed to vibrate. I was dizzy. His trousers felt rough against my thin cotton dress.

At last he spread my lids again. As he took the lens out, there was a wet sucking sound — my eye, gasping in relief when the cool air struck it. He showed me, in his terse way, how to squirt the liquid onto the lens and how to get it in, raising the right lid high and slipping the lens underneath, which I tried and did awkwardly; I had a horror of inserting foreign objects into my body. Then he told me to raise the upper lid with the index finger of my right hand and flick the lens out from below with the left index finger, quickly cupping the right hand to catch it. I tried, but couldn't get it out. It careened around in my eye, all askew. I panicked, hot and dizzy, terrified that the lens would scratch something and I would lose the little and precious vision I had in that eye. I blinked wildly and it dropped, wet and sticky, into my lap.

The doctor picked it up, cleaned it, and suggested I try again. As he watched, as I spread my lids with my fingers, I knew for certain I was violating myself, doing something perverse and masochistic, "for my own good."

The doctor outlined a complex schedule for "getting used to" the lens. I would keep it in for five minutes, three times a day, for the first three days, fifteen minutes the next three days, till eventually I could wear it all day. I loathed the progressions of self-mastery that always accompanied "getting used to" anything, and I loathed the euphemism too — if it were pleasant, there would be no need to get used to it.

No effort is greater than the effort of forcing the flesh to move in untried ways, clearing paths in the tangle of nerves to make way for an alien sensation. Even today, with all my travels, when finally I can say the word "I" without a feeling of uncertainty, I harbor a deep longing for immobility — the Brooklyn in me — an instinct at war with change and growth, those holy processes of liberal psychology. Maybe only those who have been compelled, or have compelled themselves, to travel have glimpsed the broad, unexplored terrain of human laziness — too lazy to live, some of us, yearning to lie still and sink back into primeval ooze, reversing evolution. My kind of eye, despite or perhaps because of its wandering, belongs to the genre called lazy eyes, an incarnation of the body's dearest tropism, the leaning towards more somnolent forms of life, towards death.

I was near death once — I, not the girl — and as far as I was conscious, felt that laziness pulling slowly and methodically, like the tortoise in the race, against the agile will to live and fight. How much more natural it seemed, how much easier to give in, as if giving in were what we desire all along and living is the unnatural, neurasthenic struggle. What a voluptuous numbness, how alluringly right it felt. I don't know what strength called me back — maybe just the ministrations of technology. The first eye I opened when the struggle was won, or lost, was the bad eye, and it shed a tear of utter estrangement, of long-suffering patience. The tear trickled to the corner of my lips and I tasted deep-sea brine. That eye was so powerful in the girl, in me when I was the girl, that I fear to think what would have happened had she been the one in a near-fatal accident. It might well have won. She might never have become me — I — and I would not be telling her story, my lazy eye's story.

Getting the lens in and out was as repellent as I expected, but I soon became adept at it, as I had become adept at many things that got under my skin. School, for one. The first time I inserted the lens on my own, fighting nausea, standing over the bathroom sink (no danger of its going down the drain, large as it was), I felt that slow somersault of the brain just as in first grade. So *this* is what it will be like.

I would remove the lens between classes, at the girls' room mirror, while the crowd around me puffed hastily on their cigarettes. With both eyes the same size, identical, I was a stranger to myself. My bad eye was kept in its place, its wanderings frustrated by the lens; and with its confinement, a freedom seemed to have been taken from me — no matter that the freedom to wander was accounted a blemish. With a fingertip I felt the hardness of the restraining lens beneath the veil of my upper lid. It triggered a sick lurch in my stomach that grew to a galloping, roiling fury, and this lurch and fury I never got used to.

The next Monday after school I took the subway to the doctor's office to have the lens and eye checked; no more need for my mother beside me, we agreed. I had resolved not to feel as out of place on Park Avenue as I had before, in my girlish yellow cotton dress with cap sleeves. I wore a narrow, bottle-green jersey dress usually saved for special occasions (my mother had once pronounced it "stunning" on me), and new sandals, and I put on make-up in the girls' room — my father would not let me out of the house with make-up until I reached sixteen. I had washed my hair that morning and it shone. Grownups — my parents' friends, the card players — had often teased me about my "knowing" look. Lou Zelevansky went further and joked that I had "bedroom eyes" and an "hourglass figure," phrases that made me want to squeeze my eyes shut and hide my body in a sack. I wasn't sure what a knowing look was, but I tried to assume it nonetheless, a kind of resigned, sleepy slackness of the features. In this guise I felt more of a match for Park Avenue.

It was hard to attend to what the doctor said with him leaning over me, breathing his liquory breath, his right leg at moments casually brushing against mine. But I was too wrapped in Brooklyn platitudes even to register how uneasy I felt, or why. I knew only that I found an infinity of things wrong with my life, from the commonplace — adolescence and high school and my mother's refusal to let me take two acting classes a week and the color of my eyes (that they weren't lustrous blue or green to suit my dramatic nature, but dull bedroom brown, bothered me far more than their oddity, and back then the color couldn't be changed by a lens) — to the cosmic — the uncertainty of the future and the human condition: anything except the simple fact that the doctor leaned over me too close for comfort and I didn't want to be wearing the lens or visiting his office to begin with.

For one instant, in an assault of truth that can sneak up on the most swaddled souls — like the boys at school slipping ice down the collars of our winter coats — it struck me that the doctor might be pressing his leg against mine more than necessary to examine my eye. But I dismissed this — hopped around, shook out the ice — as utter nonsense, even sacrilege, he being a grown man, a big man, on Park Avenue, and I a gauche child from Brooklyn. It was untenable; it could have opened a road to other untenable thoughts, to a universe where human nature was not as Brooklyn conspired to portray it, progressing towards ever more expansive plateaus of decency and tolerance, but rather where people were driven chaotically by impulses, everyone wanting something from everyone else and staggering about to get it. That might be the way it was in books, locked between covers, due dates stamped in the back so that they didn't even stay in your bedroom too long, but not in real life.

Going home in rush hour was a long nasty ride, crushed against sweaty strangers. I resented the trip, and the trips and checkups to follow — twice a month till I was completely "used to" the lens; "adjustments" might be needed. I had the wretched thing, I was looking normal to please my parents. Wasn't that enough? I didn't complain, though: once a process was set in motion in Brooklyn, it took more initiative to stop it than to keep it going. That was how we were; we did what we had done the day or the week before.

~

The notion that people could be driven by want rather than propriety was not entirely new to me. It was more or less what my father had said about McCarthy two years ago, that glimpse of greed and lust I had shoved behind my bad eye. Now my father's predictions were coming true — they were getting the bastard. He had had a bad summer, everyone was gloating — gone too far with his machinations, gotten himself into trouble with the Army. The sweetness of revenge by proxy was mellowed by television. He had been challenged publicly, and to my father's glee would have to submit to censure, to sticks pounding on the bucket. His days were numbered, said my father. Elections were coming up. Power would shift. Soon we would be released from his grip, like a village that has sacrificed a maiden every month to feed its resident dragon, finally released by an avenging prince.

But there was no prince. He was destroying himself — a suicidal dragon. Brooklyn had done nothing but wait. Brooklyn could maintain, unperturbed, its trust in waiting.

If only Brooklyn had been shaken to the point of revolt!

How wondrous to see crowds carrying banners through the streets, singing songs, or even tearing up the paving stones, as I had read in accounts of the Paris Commune. I was guiltily disappointed, too, that the pig had not touched anyone in Brooklyn, as far as I could tell. His victims were famous names: movie people, government people, writers. I wanted to see in the flesh, on my street, someone who had lost his job, whose furniture had been hurled down the stairs after him by a terrorized landlord, and who sat on the curb with his head in his hands, desolate, embittered, ruined. I knew this was not a nice craving, that it would horrify my mother, but I indulged it. My bad eye, growing up, was hungry for reality, famished for a scene worthy of its kind of vision.

My acting class in Manhattan also trafficked in motivations less than pure. Each Thursday afternoon eight of us, six girls and two boys, did improvisations in a bare room under the eye of a scrawny, spindly teacher with a nasal voice, who had been a great surprise the first day — I thought actors had to be handsome and sexy. He was to surprise me further, years later, by winning an Academy Award. Had I known I was in a room with someone destined for an Academy Award I might have been too intimidated even to speak; as it was I had trouble with the simple improvisations. He said we had to have a motive in each scene, something we wanted urgently. Every word we spoke, every movement, must be part of the effort to get what we wanted. Of course we needed to be quite clear in our minds about what we wanted — and that was the gist of his criticism.

"Something's not clear, Audrey. What exactly are you *after?*"

I was playing a scene with a girl who was supposed to be my mother. I was twenty-five years old, unmarried, and I ostensibly wanted to leave home and get my own place, but I didn't know how to say such an outlandish thing; maybe I wasn't certain I wanted it, either.

"Mother." I turned to her, a tiny long-haired girl named

Lizzie, from Greenwich Village. "I may as well tell you outright. I want to get an apartment of my own."

"Well, dear," she said, "that's nice. Are you sure you can afford it?"

My heart sank. Obviously this girl had never been near Brooklyn.

"Yes, I'm quite sure. You know I earn —" I cast around for a plausible sum but I didn't know what working women, usually teachers in my experience, earned. "I earn . . . enough."

"Stop, stop," implored the acting teacher. "You!" He addressed my mother. "What do *you* want?"

Lizzie shrugged. "I just want her to be happy, I guess."

"That's not enough. You have to want something of your own."

"She has to want me to stay," I said. "So I have something to fight against."

"Why should I want you to stay? Maybe I want some privacy, after all this time."

The scent of Lizzie's world breezed past the horizon of my mind, a world clearly orbs away from my own.

"This isn't working," said the acting teacher. "There's no conflict. There has to be conflict. You have to want incompatible things, urgently."

"I want to leave home urgently."

"Okay. Lizzie, help her out. You want her to stay."

"I think it might be better if you stayed home for a while, dear," said Lizzie.

"But why, Mother?"

"Well . . ." She groped vaguely at the air. "I haven't been feeling well. I need your help in the house."

"Wait a minute," I said. "Let me be the mother. I can do it."

So we switched roles. I sat down at an imaginary kitchen table.

"By the way, Mother," said Lizzie with unnerving calm,

"I've been thinking it's time I got a place of my own."

"A place of your own!" I sprang up, aghast. "What are you talking about? Since when does a young girl move out all by herself! Don't you have a perfectly good home here?"

"Of course I do. You and Dad have been great to me," she said genially. "But after all, I am twenty-five and I have a good job. We could all use some privacy at this point. I could have my friends over without disturbing you —"

"Privacy?" I shrieked. "For what, may I ask? Don't you have a lovely room? And friends? Who ever closed the door to your friends? Haven't I made them welcome, more than welcome? Twenty-five years providing a decent home for you and this is what we get!" I darted fitfully around.

"Just a minute, Audrey," the acting teacher broke in. "That has energy, that's on the right track. Except it may be a bit too much, at this point in the scene, anyway. To get to that pitch of emotion so fast there must be a strong hidden motive. Do you know what it is?"

Once I caught on, I played the scenes as life-and-death games. I was ruthlessly, obscenely tenacious.

"You're forceful, Audrey. But there's a time for understatement," said the acting teacher. "The head-on approach isn't always the most effective. Try being a little more calculating. Think of your words as part of a process, with a goal."

The next Monday I dressed in grown-up clothes again, brushed my hair, and put on make-up to go to Park Avenue, where the eye doctor leaned over me, his right leg lightly touching mine. He examined my bad eye in a new way, more inquisitively. Maybe he was trying to discover the exact nature and limits of its vision, and whether it had vision enough to see what he was after.

He must have found something — not the vision he was seeking, I didn't have that — but possibly my rampant longing to peer beneath the surfaces of things. He put his hand on my leg. I didn't move. I only looked at his hand, the fingers spread as if someone were preparing to trace them on my dress, then up at his face, which showed the strain of mental exertion, a curious diagnosis. He moved his hand up and down my leg as if feeling for something beneath the skin. He was testing, I saw that much, edging towards some crossroads where I might leap up in fear or anger, should I choose that path, or I might let the unknown happen.

As though in a dream, as though it were not a conscious act, I reached out and touched him. I touched him where I knew he would want to be touched. I know that I — she — was not the kind of girl who could do that. In my old night-time fantasies I had never touched a man that way. I was the one who was touched, gentle, romantic touches awakening me part by part. Even as I recall it, record it, I suspect I really didn't do such an outrageous thing and memory is falsifying, inventing what I wish I could have done or imagining it from what I have since become capable of doing.

Indeed this is the point at which memory may be at its least trustworthy. Things might well have stopped there and taken a different course or diffused into no course at all, into the endlessness of being sequestered in Brooklyn. It would seem much more likely that he didn't put his hand on her leg, that she only wished and feared he would. Or if he did, if I grant that he did, it seems more likely that she didn't reach out and touch him but instead stood up slowly, sliding her leg out from under his hand, which didn't move but allowed her to separate from it, then picked up her school bag and walked to the door with the tentative gliding motion of someone who fears she may be prevented or assaulted. But he wouldn't have assaulted her; probably he wouldn't even have tried to stop her, just watched her go. At home she would have told her parents fretfully that she didn't want the lens after all. It hurt. It violated her values — you can imagine by now the sorts of high-minded arguments she would have used. In the end she would have prevailed, yet felt abashed and disgusted with herself, knowing that the arguments were irrelevant, that it was only fear that kept her away.

In case that was the way it was, if she was thwarted by her fear, I must let her have it now, do it for her, since it is right that it should have happened. It suits the person I became. So I can only repeat that I did do it, unlikely as it seems. I was taken over by my bad eye, wandering.

There was little of my childhood fantasy in this reality, especially not the doctor, neither dark-skinned nor notably graceful. I could not have said whether he was good-looking or attracted me — he was a man like my father and my father's card-playing friends, the sort of man I didn't bother to look at in those terms, although my mother had pronounced him handsome despite his glasses, and admired his taste in ties.

I touched him and felt what that was like. What I touched changed under my hand, moved of its own accord, and, like the dough my mother rolled out on the kitchen table with her big wooden rolling pin, grew and solidified, which was a little frightening and at the same time made me want to giggle, there was something so absurd about it, as if he had a small doughy animal, a mouse, stretching in his trousers.

And then he did an unexpected thing — though anything he did would have been unexpected. He very gently spread my lids apart and removed the contact lens. He placed it in a saucer and took my hand like someone helping a lady from a carriage. "I think you should stand up," he said.

After he snapped the lock of the door he began caressing me, very slowly, first with his hands under my clothes and then he took off my clothes. He must have thought I knew all about it, from my touching him and from my knowing look. I did know a number of things, the facts inscribed on my blank mind by teachers, the foolish things in the wine-colored book, as well as some things hidden behind the edges of doors. But this, what he was doing to me, was not one of them. My mother claimed there was a right and wrong way to do everything. I would stay very still and accept his caresses, not daring any wrong move that could show my ignorance.

From scenes in books and movies, I thought passion always made its entrance in haste and urgency, grasping at clothing and clutching at bare flesh, panting and gasping. But this scene was languid and took time, and my body accepted and absorbed each sensation it offered with a wondrous impassivity. I was seeing such a multitude of things that there was no attention left to feel. I was all eye, the bad eye.

I had never seen a man's body except in pictures, yet that was no great surprise; it seemed something I had known all along, just as I had known how to touch him. What I hadn't had any inkling of was the immeasurable tactile reality of bodies. Suddenly the world was matter, not words. People were their bodies, not minds incidentally occupying flesh. The only other time I had been so aware of humanity as pliable flesh was the First-Aid course in junior high, those luscious manic weeks we bandaged each other, rollicking through the spring with graying rags and gauze, giddy with the feel of flesh.

But that was long ago and fleeting. I still thought knowledge could be licked off a page; daily life was a chore to be endured while the spirit waited, at one remove, to return to vivid, nourishing reality — in bed with a book on my lap. What I was doing now, though, what was being done to me, was as vivid and insistent as any book and gave the same relief of arrival at a resting place, a bedrock reality. It was even like a book, with new passages rolling through me rhythmically, each bearing its multitude of sensations, while I followed along — captive and heroine, feast and feaster — through infinitely opening spaces and elongated time. Every instant held more than seemed possible, unveiled more of the life hidden behind edges, the most startling revelation being that whole dramas could be performed in which the mind had barely any part. And as if I were turning pages with the rapt expectation of something glorious and astonishing waiting at the end, this too tantalized; I was consumed with curiosity yet wanted it to last and not reveal its ending too soon, just as in bed I needed all my powers of will not to peek ahead and spoil the last page by hastening it. Though I did not know pleasure in the common sense, that first time. That was beside the point, it could wait till later, when I was not so dazzled. I knew only the solitary pleasure of seeing beneath the surface.

The doctor, with his hairless chest, his muscled legs, his large yet fragile-looking hands, his softened and — with the glasses removed — profoundly puzzled eyes, stood up when he was done, walked nakedly to a cabinet, took out a bottle, and poured himself a drink. He offered me some but I refused. That is, I shook my head — I had hardly said a word throughout. "Do you like this?" he had whispered from time to time. "Do you like this?" And I had murmured some wordless sound. This too was altogether new — a situation where words served no purpose. Even the doctor had not used double-edged words to persuade me it was for my own good. It was for his good — I saw that with both eyes.

With my silence and acquiescence, my knowing look, he had assumed I had done this before. He discovered I had not. No wonder he was puzzled. How could he know why I went along so readily, or that my greed in its fashion was as perverse and rapacious as his own?

Staring down at me in puzzlement, he said, "Wait just a minute," which was needless — I was in no hurry to go anywhere, ready for whatever else the scene might bring. He gathered up his clothes and disappeared behind a door. I heard water running, and when he returned he was dressed, with his glasses on and an air of presiding over his office once again. I was embarrassed. I saw that I should have used the interval to get dressed too, resuming my role as patient. Very well, if that was how things were done . . . I gathered up my clothes and went into the tiny bathroom. When I came out he was sitting on the couch, bent over, head in his hands.

His shoulders jerked up and he rose to his feet. "Are you all right?"

I nodded, not sure what he meant, what being not all right would be, at this point.

"I mean, you understand, I never . . . I wouldn't have unless you seemed — I didn't mean to . . . I'm going through a very bad time —"

I wanted to stop hearing those words, which cast him in a ridiculous light. I cleared my throat, I hadn't spoken in so long. "It's all right, I'm not going to say anything."

That must have been a good answer, for his face eased and he gave a rueful smile, more befitting his role as seducer. It was the first time I had seen him smile, standing up. Standing up, he had a withdrawn manner, nothing resembling a bed-side manner. His teeth were quite nice and white. I was glad of that. I hated yellow teeth and would not have liked to think my tongue had touched yellow teeth.

"These things happen sometimes," he said. It was what my mother had said when I first asked her about my eye, long ago. He was fussing with some metal instruments on his table, the way she fussed with forks and knives when I asked her to explain, not only about my eye but about many other things in the world.

"Mm-hm," I said, as if I knew. It was just what I didn't know, how things happen, especially this thing, which apparently happened so easily, all over the place for all I knew, while I had imagined it as momentous — each time like crossing a border with armed guards and showing a pass-port — and arduous, something the body needed to antici-pate and be morally armed to undergo, like major surgery.

In Brooklyn mythology it could not happen outside of marriage, at least not to girls of fifteen who read books, though maybe to girls visibly out of bounds, the exceptionally flam-boyant (dark-eyed Carlotta Kaplowitz, ex-polio victim, had become one of those) or the exceptionally ignorant (Arlene, in my History class, "didn't know you could say no"). Ac-cording to Mrs. Carlino in her Pre-Marriage course, such creatures had no "self-respect" and their fall occurred in un-speakable circumstances. On her long-awaited Dating and

Courtship sheet, which I had in my book bag at this very moment, was the definitive meaning of Petting: "The prolonged caressing of parts of the body that do not usually come in contact before marriage."

And in romantic movies, where after the kissing and panting the scene discreetly changed, I had assumed the heroine firmly drew the line, as we were expected to do on dates. How utterly mistaken.

The world, as I stood mutely examining the doctor's flushed face, was disintegrating, to reform in another pattern. My patient bad eye, which had made me his patient, was vindicated. It had known all along how tenuous things were, how very unfreezable. It had suspected the insidious ease with which things unshaped and reshaped, constantly shifting relations so that any configuration was dissolving before the brain had seized it and locked it into a pattern of thought, sluggish brain forever lagging behind volatile world. It had known that things supposed to be hidden were right there, visible to the right eye; it was not shocked by the sight.

The way the doctor had looked at my breasts. Not like the harrowing gaze of Miss Schechter, who blinked at the raw and perilous thing I exposed. Not like the girls in the locker room after swimming class, who spoke incessantly of breasts as part of an armory of equipment, bemoaning their smallness or largeness or inefficacy of shape, or like the boys who groped for them in dark cars or on living room couches as if they were buried treasure. The eye doctor looked in a way that clarified the world — pleased, even grateful, but unamazed. Of all the ways I had dreamed the world outside Brooklyn to be, I had never conceived of its nonchalance. When he unbuttoned my dress and undid my bra — with ease, not like the boys who built fancy gadgets in shop but fumbled with the hooks of a bra — I had thought I would die of shame to be looked at. But he made it easy, all so very easy.

And the ease of this act's happening seemed something even my parents could not know about, though I was aware that they did "it" in the marriage bed — quite a different matter.

I was mistaken about many things back then, but maybe not about this: they may not have known or wanted to know how very circumstantial and arbitrary life could be, how un-programmed, how unsettled.

"I'll see you in two weeks, then?" the doctor said. I nodded. He gave me some instructions about cleaning the lens. I had forgotten all about the lens. Only when he snapped open the lock and I put my hand on the doorknob did I feel something was missing, and I stood in confusion.

"What's the matter?" He looked alarmed, as if I might suddenly make the scene he had stopped fearing.

"The lens."

"The lens?" Bafflement, then he slapped his hand to his forehead and broke out in a laugh. We had both forgotten that the lens was not in my eye or in its case in my purse but in the little saucer on his work table. He handed it to me on a tissue. I wished I could laugh at this oversight too, in a comradely way. But to display my laugh, to join it to his, would have been too intimate, too real. I accepted the lens stiffly and walked out into the waiting room. The cheerful receptionist had gone for the day and two patients were left, a young man with a bandage over one eye and an older woman wearing a black pillbox hat with a veil. I strolled past them with my head high, trying to appear blasé, a movie heroine with a shady past.

"Mrs. Daniels? You can come in now," I heard him say as he had said it to me less than an hour ago. I strolled along Park Avenue with the same casual air, as though the thing had not happened. For this, I had been schooled well.

The days proceeded in their routine way. All my waking hours I moved within the scene in the doctor's office, living over and feeling each detail and each surprise as if it were an unfathomable dream I had dreamed. And so it was with the next visit. And the next. His undressing me — after a brief check of the lens — and making love to me on the couch where my mother had perched that first day, nervously en-trusting her child to the hands of the big man, were continuing chapters of the dream, remote from the world of Brooklyn which enfolded me, though when I got home and changed my clothes I could see, I could smell the reality. I brought his smell back to Brooklyn, I thought as I stood in the shower, staring down at myself; I brought home the spouting overflow of his body and sent it down the drain.

October came and went. As the fall settled in I cultivated a new kind of double vision. My eyes were veering apart like those of the wall-eyed people in the big men's waiting rooms of my childhood, the banal left eye trained on Brooklyn, and the bad eye on the doctor's couch in Manhattan, the doctor's body weighing on mine, a scene with its skin removed, the particles barely holding together.

In mid-November the sorority interviews were held at the apartment of one of the members. The custom was to dress up, so I wore a suit and stockings and high-heeled pumps like an aspiring corporation executive, though no such ambition could then have lodged in the heart of any girl in Brooklyn. I sat gingerly on a plastic-covered sofa in a living room carpeted in sky blue, and, with the other pledges, drank tea served with the tea bag, its little paper label on a string dangling over the rim of the cup. I didn't know what to do with the tea bag, so I rested it on the edge of my saucer, where it dribbled an amber pool and slid into the center of this pool every time I lifted the cup. We were pretending to be ladies, to be our mothers, and a few sorority sisters were on hand, scrutinizing the way we managed our tea and cookies. Maybe the tea bags were left in on purpose, as a test. Most of the members were down the hall in the bedroom, where one by one the pledges would be summoned for interviews. After a while they emerged, limp, and slunk silently away.

My name was called. A girl led me to the bedroom door

and before I knew what was happening, tied a scarf around my eyes. I heard jabbering on the other side of the door, but when I was led in it subsided to an absolute stillness, as our voices in the school auditorium were stilled by a warning chord on the piano. Sightless, I was guided to a hard straight chair. I must have been in the center of the room; I felt space at my back. I wanted to reach out to find a wall, place myself in relation to something firm, but I reined in the impulse.

"We understand, Audrey, that you want to be a member of Chi Delta Epsilon. Is that right?"

"Yes."

"How much do you want it?"

"Well, I really do want to . . . I'm not sure what you mean by how much."

"We mean, how far would you be willing to go for it?"

Each question came from a different voice, as if these were lines read from a script, and the voices were disguised — I couldn't identify them. I kept turning my head in the direction of each voice; one was definitely behind me. Where could placid, reliable Susan be? Could she really be a part of this?

"Well, it depends . . ."

"Maybe if we ask you some questions . . . For instance, if the sorority asked you to dye your hair green, would you do it?"

"Dye my hair green? I don't . . . If everyone else did, maybe . . . just for a while . . ."

"Do you mean to say you're that much of a conformist?"

These were not the kinds of questions I had expected (hobbies, ambitions, favorite movie stars) or knew what to do with. There must be better answers, correct answers, if only I could figure them out.

"I didn't say that. It would depend what for . . ."

"If a sister cheated on an exam, would you report her?"

"It would depend . . . Well, I guess not. I'd probably mind my own business."

"Do you mean to say you don't believe in honesty? That you approve of cheating?"

It continued in this vein for an eternity. I grasped that it would have no natural parabola but would continue until they decided to stop. The image I had lived with for so long had come to life. Not a bucket but a blindfold, not evil communists but schoolgirls. Why should I be shocked? I myself had given it life by harboring and nurturing it so long, and then stupidly surrendering to it. My insides churned. I had succumbed to Brooklyn and look where it led . . . And it was all so unnecessary: a year from now I would be gone, far from Brooklyn. The Sorbonne . . .

"Have you ever been on a bed with a boy?"

I snapped back to attention, to my school attitude. There had to be a right answer, just figure out what they want. "Yes" could mean I was daring and independent, or else a slut. "No" could mean I was respectable or comically inexperienced. I didn't know these girls well enough to be sure — it might turn on their whim of the moment. There was also the matter of truth itself. Had I? Strictly speaking, no. I had endured the usual ventures at parties when the lights were turned down, but surely they weren't what my questioners had in mind.

Literal truth was what my mother seemed to value. Wasn't that what she meant by "To thine own self be true"? And wasn't she, with her sensible brown eyes, the incarnation of standard vision, the supremely reliable index of what the world at large wished of me?

Not for a moment had I forgotten the eye doctor or what happened in his office; all of that was sealed behind the bad eye, which took it in. But the eye doctor was not only in a different world, in the stellar reaches of Park Avenue — he was not a boy and it was not a bed we lay on but a brown leather couch, on which, after the first time, he spread a sheet because the leather was uncomfortable on bare skin, especially slick with sweat.

I confessed that, no, I had never been on a bed with a boy.

No giggles, no further questions. Just an inscrutable midnight silence lasting so long that every muscle in my body went rigid. I was blinded, encircled: they could do anything they pleased, stone me or set on me like savages, pulling my hair and tearing at my clothes.

Someone stepped up from behind and touched my shoulder. I jumped. She led me across the room and out the door, closing it behind us. In the hall, she removed the blindfold and light smacked my eyes. It was the same girl who had taken me in, a Carol. Colored spots surrounded her face like a halo. I blinked. My right eye probably wandered a bit, seeking solace after its imprisonment. As my vision cleared so did the sober pink face of Carol, who told me to leave without speaking to any of the other girls. I would be notified of the decision early in the week.

The next day, a Monday, I went up to see the eye doctor. I was used to him by now, as I was used to the lens, which I could keep in for hours at a stretch. I had learned to enjoy what he did to me, too, but when I first cried out he had touched my open mouth with his fingers and said, "Shh, they'll hear you." Not harshly. In the tone of an experienced person cautioning a younger one, precisely the case, and precisely my mother's tone. And so along with learning pleasure I learned not to be too loud about it, even in the wide absorbent spaces of Manhattan.

This Monday, as every other, he dressed in the bathroom. When he came out his face had a subdued version of the look that accompanied his orgasms — unsettled, distraught, bordering on panic. I knew it well. I watched. Through half-closed lids I watched him.

I was still lying on the couch. I was always bemused afterwards; each time there was something slightly different, something I could not have imagined, for I didn't have a lascivious imagination — I was a more bookish sort of dreamer. Not that I still believed everything I read in books. In all my afternoon hours with the eye doctor, the dread words in the old wine-colored book had never been uttered, and we had gone far beyond the boundaries of its instructions. Nothing we had done, except in the most general sense, even resembled its instructions. (Nothing I ever did since, either.) I sat on his hips and his chest and his shoulders, but never on his lap. Neither of us could have managed that. That was a forbidden border.

Today, while we lay on the couch, he had nudged me over onto my stomach and climbed on top of me. I was confused. I remembered the day we celebrated the end of the war, and how the black dog alongside the country road, also celebrating, balanced on his hind legs as he did it to the indifferent gray terrier. And class trips to the zoo, where the purple-bottomed apes clambered over each other as I purpled with embarrassment myself, not so much for what they were doing as for that savage color they exposed.

He urged me to lift myself up and fitted himself inside me. I was pierced with shame. I might not be the delicate bride of the manual, yet I was part of her species: it was inconceivable for her to be balancing on her knees, with her shoulders low and her breasts hanging down like udders, presenting her secret parts to the light like those purple apes. I did it, though. In his office I did the inconceivable. And as it went along I let myself sink, pressed down into the strangeness of it, till I saw and felt what was beneath still another surface. Interesting; everything about this subterranean rite, the great human secret, was powerfully interesting, except this way I couldn't watch his face.

Lying there musing while he dressed, I almost drifted off to sleep.

"I'm sorry to keep sending the bills." His voice roused me. "I don't like to, you know, but your parents would wonder . . ."

I said nothing. What were bills to me? Only the papers on my father's little desk, to be processed and torn across and thrown in the wastebasket. My parents didn't discuss money in front of me, though I knew we were not rich, not even "comfortable": they would never have consulted a Park Avenue doctor for anything but the most urgent of remedies. For all I knew they might be making sacrifices so that I could visit the eye doctor twice a month.

"Do you understand?" he said.

"I understand." I didn't fully understand, but I felt something shaping vaguely in my mind, a blur set in motion by his mentioning my parents. It was an amorphous image of this situation as it might be viewed from the world outside his office. It had never had a shape before; it was fluid, unreeling like a tide of silk from a hidden spool, in this closed room, for me alone. Now it was struggling to form itself into a pattern like other sequential events in the world, a story with a plot that need not take a random path but might be designed. An opportunity, a dim byway in the plot, seemed to be opening. But I couldn't conjure up the pattern all on my own. He had to say something more first.

"I really do need to keep checking for about another month and a half. After that it wouldn't be fair . . ." He paused for a response, but as usual I could think of nothing to say. "I never know what you're thinking," he burst out, dashing his hand over his head as if to smooth something down. Maybe his hair had been unruly, when it was thicker. "You never say anything."

He was right. In his office I cultivated a silence as impenetrable as the chicken flicker's. Bobby's mother. She couldn't speak, and I wouldn't. I had always admired her silence, or rather her ability to live and move in silence, while I used words to reassure myself that my life was truly happening. Now, with no effort, I was in possession of that power. It didn't feel like power. Was the world, I wondered, as stupefying to Bobby's mother as the scenes in the eye doctor's office were to me?

"Are you all right, Audrey? What do you think about all this? About me?"

Thanks to my father and the evening news, I knew what the Fifth Amendment was. You didn't have to answer if your answer might get you into trouble.

"Say something. Please."

He was pleading. I said the first thing that came into my head. "I'm still a child. I don't have to think anything."

He froze in astonishment. "Of course you have to think. Everyone has to think. I think about it. I don't do this with everyone who walks in here, you know. Do you suppose I do?"

I had never thought about that one way or the other. I never thought of him apart from myself, what his life or habits might be, whether he had been born anywhere and had a history. (Not with everyone who walked in, certainly. That was out of the question.) I thought about me, about how I might escape from Brooklyn and what I would find in the world. Outside of the time we spent in his office the doctor was an abstraction and might not have existed. He simply happened to me. He sprang out of nothingness that day in September when he opened the door and beckoned.

"Don't you ever wonder what could make me do this? Don't you realize this is as bizarre for me as it is for you?"

It was the word "bizarre" that reached me. No one had ever used it to me in conversation. It was a word from my fantasy conversations with the people I would know in later life, real life. For the first time, I spoke to him in my truthful voice. "Oh, no," I said. "I don't think that's possible."

"Christ, you don't get it at all, do you? You don't see . . . Something happened when you first sat down here, I don't know what it was, the way you looked, maybe, so far away and contained, yet so frightened. So beautiful, or almost . . . on the verge of it, any minute you might be beautiful. It was better the minute before. Your cheeks were burning hot, I guess it was terror, I could feel the heat coming off them. I don't know, it set something off. I swear to you I never did anything like this, I mean with anyone so young. And a patient. You don't realize the risk — I have a family — you don't realize I'm obsessed! I think about you all the time, with my other patients, with my wife . . . It's as if I carry you around with me, I can't get you out of my head and yet in a way I don't even know you, it's a kind of madness . . ." He stumbled into the patient's chair I usually sat in and hung his head, making an awful gulping noise. "I count the days till you come. Can you understand how humiliating it is for a grown man to feel this way about a — a — practically a child? Do you know there are moments when I want to steal you away, run somewhere with you — there's something in you I have to have. My God, it's like some awful thing you read in the papers . . ."

On he went, and I sat opposite him, naked, compelled to hear. I wanted to cover my ears but that was infantile and wouldn't help anyway — the words would keep breaking on me in waves, only muffled. It was like being possessed, he said, he knew the situation was impossible but he was a prisoner, I drove him wild, he was drowning in it, he even named unmentionable parts of my body and what they made him feel, which made me want to die of shame, for it was one thing to do it and another to say it — all of it in disjointed phrases that I recognized from reading great books as the worst kind of banalities. Had he known me in the slightest he would have prepared something elegant and literary.

His words assaulted in waves and I was washed under them. I was out beyond my depth, I who had no perception of depth. If I kept listening I would drown with him. I yearned to be home with the blankets around me, reading a book. If only I had some clothes on. My bare skin was the target of his words, absorbing them like accusations. Maybe I was supposed to apologize, but I didn't know what I had done. I had done only what he wanted.

"I wish I could do something for you," he said more quietly. The spurt of madness was ebbing, thank God. His voice got tight, as if it had to squeeze itself out past something impossible to swallow. "I feel I should."

In the midst of drowning I glimpsed it, a piece of driftwood. My moment, my plot opening. Something hidden and unsuspected sprang out of me to clutch it. Not the Sorbonne — that would be like asking for the moon. "I want to take another acting class. Scene Study."

"Acting class?"

Naturally he was bewildered. I never told him what I did after school, or in it, for that matter. Or anything at all. But I knew it would make no difference. And I wanted it. I had learned how to want with a vengeance.

"Yes, I'm going to be an actress." I decided that instant, as the words formed.

I was prepared for an ironic comment of the sort I might get from my father. But he simply asked me how much I would need. As I figured it out silently, my mother stirred within me, her fine housewifely efficiency and grasp of the uses to which things could be put. I named the exact sum, no extras, no carfare.

"I'll write you a check." He opened his desk drawer.

"No. What would I do with a check? I told you, I'm a child."

"Sorry. Of course. Cash, then. That way is better for me too."

I nodded.

He reached into his back pocket.

I accepted the bills but had nowhere to put them. They lay in my open palm, against my bare thigh. Months ago, from our porch, my mother had watched as a boy from down the block gave me two dollars. When I came up the steps she told me never to take money from men on the street. Laughing at her, I explained he had borrowed it to buy lunch, but she stood firm: no matter what it was for, it just didn't look right. This wasn't the street, though.

"I have to go home." I got up and looked around for my purse.

"I know you must be upset by what I've said. I'm sorry, Audrey. Maybe I shouldn't have spoken, but —" He reached for me but I evaded him. He might start all over again. I took my things into the bathroom, dressed quickly, and fled.

On the way to the subway I paused at the church. I had passed it so many times before and never stopped: the spell of the eye doctor's office began and ended at the subway steps and I could not heed anything else along the way. But today felt different. I paced around it, taking in the curves and planes of the warm stone, squinting a bit to see how the contours would dissolve and reassemble. Through my right eye it looked like the jagged, shakily balanced still lifes in the museum a few blocks away, where my adventurous girlfriend who found the acting class had once taken me. It teetered on its foundations, a sinuous pile of stones strung like beads.

The message on the signboard said: "The Church is a haven of rest for all. Come in and refresh your spirit." I wondered if that could mean me too. Wasn't I part of "all"?

"All" meant you didn't have to stop and think it over. I pushed open one of the immense double doors and went in, tiptoeing down the center aisle. I had never seen such high and grand inner spaces except in Radio City Music Hall, where my mother took a party of girls for my twelfth birthday — though what I remembered most about that outing was the man masturbating in the little platform between the subway cars, rubbing himself industriously with thumb and forefinger through the fabric of his pants. He had caught my eye but I looked away and pretended I hadn't seen.

Late afternoon light filtered through stained glass windows, dappling the marble fonts and great stone pillars and statues along the side walls with patches of rainbow. Up in front was an altar decked with mounds of red and yellow flowers. The burnished mahogany pews were orderly and serene. Three people sat scattered far apart. I returned to the back and slid into the last row.

I had never been in a church before. Entering, actually sitting down, was the most alien and forbidden thing I had ever done. I could sooner have told my mother that I slept with the eye doctor than that I had gone into a church to refresh my spirit. She would have judged it high treason, and somewhere in her rebuke would have come the words "To thine own self be true."

This was their holy place, I knew, where people came to worship the man born in that inexplicable way (nonsense, my father said) and then sacrificed in that horrible way, for which we were unjustly held responsible. Therefore you could not trust any of them, my father said, and what they had done to us in the war was too awful even to be spoken of. A riddle: we must keep it in mind always and forever but never speak of it. Why was it that things so real in their savagery that your heart rocked in its cradle of blood at the mere thought of them, must never be spoken of?

Yet here I was in their sanctuary, a traitor and trespasser. It should have felt very wrong; I waited for the familiar Brooklyn shame to prickle my skin but nothing happened. It was so alluring here, and the allure so remote from anything like God or the war. It was simply the place itself, the size, the emptiness, the light. For the first time in memory, I was in a place — a haven — where no one could get at me, and that was holiness enough. It was all the holiness I needed at fifteen.

I gave my spirit leave to be refreshed. Vast as they were, the vaulted spaces around me expanded, till at last there was space enough to breathe in. I took huge breaths of stillness and calm, as though I had never breathed my fill before. That such a place existed and I had found it, a place to be alone and true to one's self, made me flush with intimations of possibility. Maybe all of life need not be "getting used to" things I dreaded. Maybe there was another way to live it, some free and unhampered way I could recover from those years before I stood waiting on the ration lines gripping my mother's hand, before I began school and was assigned a place in the ranks. Like old springs cramped for eons in a tiny space, my feelings slowly uncoiled, and as they uncoiled, spread a blossoming misery through me. Confusions wound out of me like snakes squirming and stretching at my feet. In this vast space I could admit what was not admissible in Brooklyn: how unhappy I was. Had I told my mother I was unhappy she would have replied that I was mistaken, that I, so young and so fortunate — simply to have been born safely on this soil was fortunate — could have no idea what real unhappiness was.

From the mere naming of it sprang a passionate elation, and I wished never to leave the church. I could sleep in the pews, go out and scavenge for food, and spend the days in blissful contemplation of the miseries I was denied at home. It would be ages before they found me.

But they would, in the end. I was not free, I was still a child. I had to return to Brooklyn, though I knew, just as certainly as I knew the source of my elation, that the moment I stepped out on the street my confusions would writhe their way back inside me.

I trudged up the aisle and leaned my body on the great door. In the gathering darkness outside, streaked with white shards from the streetlights, my eye teared under the lens.

I couldn't tell how long I had stayed in the church, but the subway was more crowded than ever before — rush hour at its peak. I had to stand on the little platform between the cars, crushed by businessmen in suits, carrying briefcases. I hardly minded, I was so dazed, dreaming of my future life in faraway places that seemed newly attainable and welcoming, glimmering with silvery adventure, when I thought I felt something moving high on the back of my left leg. I stiffened. It circled on my thigh, exploring a small tender area with immense concentration and patience. I tried to move but there was nowhere to go. I glanced furtively at the men near me, to connect faces with hands, but we were packed so tight, sticking together like raisins in a box, that it could have been any one of three or four or, I tried to hope, no one at all, an innocent jiggling briefcase.

It was becoming an effort to draw breath. I must do something. What would a sensible person like my mother do to make it stop? She would turn to the most likely man and say loudly, "Get your hands off me!" The prospect was appalling; I was not capable of it. What if I picked the wrong one? I would die of shame, with no place to run. I felt guilty already at the thought of a wrong accusation. And all the while the hand, the fingers, moved along my thigh.

It was an express train. Local stations where I might have escaped whizzed cruelly by. The trip would never end; before it ended I would break into parts like those Cubist paintings. This couldn't be happening, it was too vile, it was probably not a hand at all, I was imagining it — my own dirty mind, corrupted, while on the outside I still looked like a decent schoolgirl. How on earth could any of these ordinary businessmen wish to do something so pointless on a subway? The very idea was absurd. Unless they could tell by looking at me. Could it show? My parents didn't see it. Maybe only certain kinds of people . . . I tried again to force myself through the packed bodies but it was impossible. If only I could faint. I could pretend to faint. In movies fainters closed their eyes and went demurely limp, then people picked them up and fanned them and gave them brandy, but it was so crowded here that no one would notice. I would suffocate under their feet.

To make the stations move on, I set my mind little goals: the capitals of all the states, the periodic table of the elements, lines of poetry ("Two roads diverged in a yellow wood / And sorry I could not travel both . . ."), but I had to abandon each one, I couldn't concentrate; and all the while the hand moved around and around and I sneaked looks at the men near me, ashamed to face them directly, as if I were doing something atrocious. I noticed one on my left wearing a light brown fedora with a dark brown band. His little blue eyes seemed made of porcelain, dainty yet hard, and they stared straight ahead. His tight lips and double chin were lines painted on the rosy blob of his face. But maybe I was doing him an injustice. Would the hand never have enough? How long could it make those same circuits? I knew a bit about men now, the tenacity of their wants, the ecstatic monotony of repetition, but all that knowledge was in Manhattan, while right this minute the train was burrowing its way to Brooklyn where I was just a girl, I didn't really know anything, please stop, leave me alone, I'm not what you think, it's all a mistake.

At last the train dragged into a station and I bored my way out. I shot a fierce look at the porcelain-eyed man. His face didn't change a jot. On the platform I smoothed out my dress. Surely the fingers had left tracks on my body, grooves that would stay for life and that everyone would see, with their vaunted depth perception.

At home I found a note, hand-delivered, my mother said, by one of the sorority girls. "We regret to inform you . . . This is no reflection on . . . work out for the best, in the long run." Naturally. I should have known. I had not told the truth at the interview. I had quibbled over words like a Jesuit, to justify a lie, or a rather significant omission. Nor had I been true to myself, and that, I decided, was the real reason I had been rejected. The sorority sisters, with their unflawed binary vision, had seen right through to the depths of me — to my scorn and my secrets — and pronounced judgment.

My mother tried to console me. Don't feel bad. It wasn't important enough to waste my feelings on — as if I had a limited supply. These were ignorant girls who had no right to judge me and anyway could not appreciate me. I was "different."

I always shrank in my skin on hearing that word, "different." Not because I wanted to be like others — I wanted others to be like me. Yet I was grateful for her loyalty. I was swept by a rush of love. I wanted to fall on her neck and sob and tell her what had happened on the subway, and be stroked and soothed and assured this would never happen again, and hear her righteous fury at the bad man. But how could I? What happened on the subway seemed connected to my going into the church and to the eye doctor and the money and the acting class, none of which I could ever tell her about. I saw my oracular mother diminish before my eyes and become useless; I could never tell her anything again because everything was connected to everything else in a way only my bad eye could grasp. And even though she might understand if I could bring myself to explain the connections, they were gossamer connections, a web that would fall into shreds if I pressed it too hard for logic and meaning, compressed it into outline form. Besides, I wouldn't know how or where to begin, how to invent a language of connections. There were barriers, thickets of ignorance and confusion in both of us that I would have to hack my way through to arrive at the clearings of understanding. It was simply too hard to do, the distance to cover was too great. I would have to remain alone in the midst of it. We would never see the same thing or occupy the same landscape. In the end, this longing to have her see through my eyes, just once to feel how the world looked and felt to me, would be forever frustrated.

When she grew old she developed a partial blindness peculiar to the old, though in some cases, her doctor said, it could begin as early as forty. In this ailment, some sadistic metaphor of the gods, the vision dims and blurs at the center, leaving the victims to see a fuzzy sphere of indistinct gray bordered by a brighter, articulated penumbra of reality. They cannot see what is right in front of them, only peripheries; they recognize things by the fluttery outlines. They cock their heads, peer and squint to get around the edge of the central vacuum, catch the bright ring and yank it back to the center by the rays of the eye, but the bright world eludes them, forever on the teasing edge.

I tried to help her. I sought remedies — photographers' lights, jewelers' magnifying glasses, even elaborate machines with lighted screens for reading. Every time I saw her I brought a new toy. See, Mother! You must try to see! But she accepted no help. The remedies were all too difficult to get used to. She accepted the darkening at the center of things. It was an obsession with me to make her see, make her, by any contrivance, want to see. But I failed. Maybe it was wrong to try, as it is wrong to interfere with anyone's vision. And God, how I envied and scorned her vision when she had it — so focused, so suitable, so thoroughly useful. Then it dragged her down into the dark.

She kept on with her soothing words but I interrupted, shouting that the rejection had nothing to do with my eye, either, because I had been wearing the lens at the interview, the lens she wanted me so badly to have, and see? it hadn't served the slightest purpose. I was no more acceptable with it than without. So there. She looked so pained that I was wretched over my outburst and too ashamed to tell her I had actually been blindfolded at the interview. Perhaps that was a mitigating fact, but I was not sure what it mitigated. My mother would have been appalled to know they had required and I had submitted to the blindfold; she would have said her usual words.

No matter. It served her right to be denied the truth. It was all her fault that I had turned out the way I did. If she had not handed me over so promptly and obediently to the authorities the minute she had me, if she had watched over what they did to me, my eyes would have been ordinary and seen things in the ordinary way. I would have been content to live in Brooklyn and settle.

I ran upstairs to take a shower and collapse on my bed, where I relived the scene with the eye doctor. Those mortifying words about my body, what it did to him . . . That my humdrum girl's body, the most familiar thing in the world, not me but the thing that contained me, could enthrall him, was outrageous. I had never been outraged about what he did to me, but this was different, full of danger. He had no right to *feel* that way about me. He said he was possessed, but I had no wish to possess him. Children, in Brooklyn mythology, were blank slates, not possessing anything, not responsible for anything. Hadn't my own mother brought me there to have him breathe his hot breath on me and brush his leg on mine?

His words might be banal; their force was not. I sensed

where it could lead. It was starting already, a tug behind my ribs. I was on the verge of caving in to it, contracting my body around the central core like a dancer rounding to a passionate crescent, on the verge of feeling something myself for the eye doctor — whether pity or contempt or love or loathing mattered less than that it was feeling. He, *it,* would become part of my real life, and from this moment on, if I wanted to be true to myself, *that* would be part of what I must be true to.

My eye ached; I wasn't ready to keep the lens in for so long. I took it out, standing over the bathroom sink. In the palm of my hand it became a jellyfish. I flinched from the sting. In the small, windowless bathroom something of the aura of the church returned to me, the space to think a free and true thought: how ugly the lens was and how I hated it. Even more, more than anything else, I wanted never to take that subway ride again.

If I never went back, the eye doctor would cease to exist. My visits would have served their purpose and could be left behind like the improvisations we did in acting class. Weren't my scenes with the eye doctor, self-contained, circumscribed in time, also improvisations in their way? In that light, I had been a very poor actress. I hadn't played them with any energy — "energy" being a word the spindly acting teacher used often — because I wasn't sure what I wanted. Perhaps I had gotten what I wanted and there was no point in repeating the scene. It "didn't work," as we said in acting class.

I wrapped the lens in a tissue and flushed it away. As it vanished in the swirl of water my right eye teared with joy.

Sometimes during spells of pain you can wake in the morning drenched with freedom and light and well-being, and this lasts a few glorious seconds while your life waits, like a resplendent party, a gala, for you to make your entrance. Eager to rise and put on your finery, you linger just an instant on the threshold, anticipating — when the pain comes up from behind like a sneak and grabs you. Back in its familiar embrace, you know that all along it was lurking in the folds of the sheets and you were only toying with freedom, allowing yourself to be deceived, and the light and well feeling which a moment ago filled the room evaporates like dew.

The next few mornings were that way. I woke from the sweet, dense sleep of the young, ready to suck the juice of the world as I would an orange, and then the story I had tried to shape closed around me: the man on the subway, the eye doctor and his terrifying words, the lens and what to tell my parents — for eventually I would have to tell them it was gone, it was all over with perfecting me.

Only my bad eye took no part in my worries. As always, it went its blithe way, following its desires. Light and air stroked it, a forever fresh, unencumbered eye, an explorer.

Days passed. I was swimming three times a week in school — no one graduated without taking the rigorous swimming test, though a number graduated semi-literate — and under the spicy green water, the world far away, I found another kind of haven. Most of the body was water, the chemistry teacher had once said. To be water was to be fluid and elusive, nothing could grab you. I was at one with my water self, safe in my element.

And falling asleep at night, recalling not the eye doctor himself but the things he had done to me, I relaxed and almost convinced myself that my problem would go away. My parents would forget. Especially my father. He had never said much about the lens; probably he was unaware of the stages of my getting used to it, occupied as he was with the things in his department. Except that he paid the bills — the same day he got them, as I knew from watching years ago, sitting on his lap at the little desk. And the eye doctor would stop sending bills: hadn't he said it wouldn't be fair . . . ?

The days accumulated. A week. Two weeks. Each time

my eyes met my mother's I waited to be called to account, but she never said a word. I looked her straight in the eye on purpose, testing my nerve and testing her too. Did she ever really look at me?

On the Monday of my regular appointment with the eye doctor, I went to the library after school, taking care to arrive home at the time I usually returned from his office. My mother was cleaning the broiler. We had an electric broiler now, and seldom used the one below the oven, which had erupted in flames of grief the day Roosevelt died. I rummaged in the refrigerator for milk, milk that no longer wore little wires around its neck as it had during the war, and that no longer needed to be shaken up — it was homogenized by machine. Even the milk had settled, or maybe just grown up. We kept shaking, though, out of habit.

My mother turned to me, placing her hands on her hips. "And where were you this afternoon?"

The tone and the combative stance meant this was a moment for truth telling.

"The library."

"The library!" As if I had said the pool hall or the opium den. "Well, the eye doctor called," she announced.

"Mm."

"He sounded worried. He wanted to know why you didn't show up. He called himself, not his secretary."

"Mm-hm."

"What is this mm-hm? Why didn't you go? What's the matter with you?"

"I didn't feel like it." I spilled some milk as I poured. She rushed over with a damp rag before I could set the bottle down.

"What do you mean, you didn't feel like it? This isn't something you do because you feel like it. If it has to be checked, you go whether you feel like it or not."

"I don't want to wear it. It hurts. I never wanted it in the first place."

"Oh, you didn't? Now you tell me! You might have thought of that before we spent all that money. Not to mention the trips I made back and forth."

"Two trips," I breathed.

"Whatever. Why didn't you say something then? You don't seem to have too much difficulty opening your mouth."

"You never gave me a chance. It was just decided. You're the one it bothered, that I wasn't perfect. I never cared. Who needs to be perfect?" She was silent, a silence so magnetic that it pulled out my words: "I'll never be perfect now anyway."

The skin around her mouth and eyes tightened — her canny look. I could sense the cells of her brain drawing together with energy.

"Just a minute. Hold everything." She pulled out a plastic kitchen chair and sat. "Something is fishy here. Sit down and tell me what's going on."

I backed away towards the door.

"I never said you had to be perfect, Audrey. You know we love you the way you are. We were doing this for your own good. I thought you understood that. We thought, now you were at an age when it could make a difference, when it might be easier when you get to college — "

"Oh, who cares about all that! Boys, dates. Believe me, it's not eyes they're interested in. You don't need twenty-twenty vision to have some creep want to put his hands all over you. And who ever said I wanted to be popular and get married and settle down and play mah jongg?"

"Don't you talk to me that way! And don't raise your voice to me either!"

I ignored that. "You didn't even notice I wasn't wearing it. That's how much difference it makes. You never looked at me long enough or hard enough to notice. You don't understand anything about me. You don't have the slightest idea." I burst into tears and rushed to fall on her neck as I had longed to do two weeks ago.

"My poor baby." She stroked my hair as I sobbed. "What could be happening that's so terrible? Of course I notice you. Don't you think I know you? I know all about you. I know you're different. Now don't cry. Don't feel that way. Tell me what it is. Is it something at school? Those nasty girls again?"

I shook my head. My composure was returning. Whenever I heard that word, "different," every organ got taut.

"Then what? You can tell me."

"It's too awful."

"You'd better tell me, Audrey, if it's that awful."

I had gone much too far. Luckily I had something suitable to tell her. I offered, haltingly, the episode of the man on the subway. He too had his uses.

"Ugh!" She thrust me from her to look at my face. "It's disgusting. It never fails. You can't go through life without something like that . . . Look, sweetheart, there's not a woman I know who hasn't had that happen at least once. It's part of being a woman. Men can be animals, it's the honest truth. You have to fight back. Let them know you won't stand for it."

"It was too crowded." I wept again. The telling of it, and her response, revived the horror. That it happened to everyone made it worse, not better.

"It's all right, Audrey. I don't mean you did anything wrong. You're young, how could you know? Listen to me. Right now it seems very important. But you'll see, time will pass, it'll fade away. It doesn't mean anything in the long run. I thought maybe something *really* awful had happened." Relief triumphant. She tried a little chuckle to lighten things, but this was premature, for just as she was saying it meant nothing, I was feeling his heavy fingers on my thighs. I squirmed in her tight embrace.

"And you've been walking around for two weeks with this weighing on you. Why didn't you tell me before?"

I extricated myself and blew my nose.

"I know. You were embarrassed. But you can tell me these things, Audrey. I'm a married woman. I know what men are like. Don't worry that I'll be shocked." She had my anguish, which always threatened to become her own, under control now. Like a potter, she could twist the raw, earthy material around in her hands, taming it until it grew manageable. Soon she would have this so small and shapely that she could tell her mah jongg friends about it. Together they would nod and frown, and maybe recall similar incidents long ago in their own lives, and laugh a bit. They could domesticate anything.

Finally I started to drink my milk.

"I better call the eye doctor and explain to him," she said.

"No!"

"Don't worry. I won't tell him that. I'll just say you couldn't make it, you didn't feel well."

"No, don't. Please."

"Don't be silly, Audrey. I promised to call back and let him know. I won't say anything to embarrass you." She went to the phone at my father's desk in the dining room. Through the doorway I could see her looking up the number. "You young girls are so sensitive," she said as she began dialing.

I took a sip of milk but had to spit it back. There was something large, like an egg, in my throat, and when I tried to swallow, the egg corked my body. My mother and the eye doctor were actually going to speak to each other. This was a cosmic impossibility, like day and night occurring at once, or having each foot planted on a different continent.

I heard the ordinary words, real and unmistakable. "Audrey didn't feel well at school . . ."

Hearing them on the other end, equally real, filling in her pauses, was that person who touched me in secret places, who said he loved me and thought about me constantly, and whom I had expected to vanish conveniently when I had had enough of him, as characters vanish when you slam a book shut. He would have vanished, too. It was my mother who insisted on resurrecting him.

"She stayed on at the nurse's office until they felt she might be sent home."

When she spoke to outsiders my mother employed a more elegant and complex syntax than she did for family members, like dressing up to go out. She had a number of finely tuned variations: her unrefined, serviceable idiom for household use, something more sharply honed for her friends, and more self-conscious for the teachers at school. For the world outside Brooklyn there was this stylish, subjunctive-laden mode. Her versatility carried over into Yiddish too, which she threw out in short pithy remarks to my father around the house, but spoke to my grandmother in fluent and elaborate phrases. The strange sounds used to catapult them both over a border, out of my reach, until I realized that without even trying to understand, despairing of understanding, I knew what they were saying. How this happened was incomprehensible. In English, which I floated in as I floated in water, my element, I knew the nature and function and potentialities of every word and every inflection. I had no idea, in my mother's and grandmother's Yiddish, what the words were one by one, or even when one word ended and another began — it was a steady flow of syllables like the flow of the chicken flicker's vowels, though far more rhythmic and civilized — yet at the end of the inscrutable journey of sentence or paragraph, miraculously I had arrived, which made it less a language than a form of subliminal transport, a direct delivery of thought and feeling.

This virtuosity of hers boasted of an enviable comfort in the ordinary world, an instinctive sense of degrees of propriety, a subtle economy of means. While I had only one language — my brand of stubborn integrity — and it had awkwardly to fit all circumstances.

No wonder I had to master all phases of language later on, and wanted to speak other people's words on a stage, to become promiscuous in every idiom and escape every sort of purity. And then others' words proved not enough and I had to learn to speak the languages of both my eyes and invent other I's to speak through, even this very I speaking now — to be certain no form of vision was denied me, and by an alchemy of the imagination, to turn vision into speech.

Hugging the phone to her ear, my mother paused. I imagined the doctor's voice: aloof, concerned.

"No, nothing serious," she replied, and in a lower tone — though it was hardly possible for me not to hear, I was eight feet away — went on, "I think this experience with the lens has been something of a strain on her. I didn't realize to what extent . . . Yes, certainly, I'll tell her that. And I'm awfully sorry to have inconvenienced you."

She was apologizing! I could barely breathe. The egg in my throat grew steadily larger, blocking off my body from my brain. I cast about for what to say when she hung up.

"Yes, she's right here. Audrey dear, the doctor would like to speak to you."

"What for?"

She covered the mouthpiece with her palm. "How should I know? Just come here and talk to him. And behave yourself."

I took the phone. She stood at my side.

"Audrey? I was frantic when you didn't come. Are you all right?"

I moved a few steps off. "Yes, fine. Thank you," I added, so that my mother would see I knew how to behave.

"You know what I mean. Nothing's happened? Nothing's wrong?"

What did he think could have happened? Here I was. He sounded as silly as my parents when I stayed out late. "No, nothing."

"You haven't said anything to your mother, have you?"

"No."

"Audrey, don't leave like this. Please. I have to see you. We must talk."

My mother was watching me in her telepathic mode, trying to instill the right answers, though this time she didn't even know the questions. I mimed a look of impatience, rolling my eyes at his tedious doctorly concern. An unnecessary precaution. It was beyond her imagining — a doctor, a big man. Even I could not have imagined this — his pleas in my ear as my mother gazed on stolidly, praying I would not disgrace her further by crude manners.

"I'm not sure."

"Yes. Next week. You'll feel better once we talk. I know you're upset and confused. At least let me speak to you."

"I'll have to see." I hung up.

"Well," said my mother. "If you had told me right away what happened on the subway we could have avoided all that. I would have gone with you if you wanted. Anyhow, I told him you'd be there next week. He'll make time for you. Look, I know it's not easy getting used to the lens, but once you are, you'll see it's for the best, in the long run."

I had always been puzzled by those words, "in the long run," rhythmic twin to "for your own good." So much of my time was invested in this famous long run — when would it ever begin? I might have amassed so many burdens by then that I wouldn't be able to run at all. Weren't there any short runs? Or were they sucked in and annihilated by the longer run, like stellar matter in a black hole? Definitely what I did in the doctor's office was for the short run — done for its own sake, over when it was over. Was it for that unabashed self-containment that the short run was slightly disreputable? And yet while it lasted, time leaped alive out of its turgid preparatory trudge. The short run left memories, too. Were they for the long run, making the short run a kind of energetic servant, proxy for an ancient master too gouty and pompous to run on his own? If the long run was made of memories, then I had better do lots of things in the short run, storing them up.

(This, now, is the long run. I found it. I'm in it. I run with my story, stored up so long, scattering it before me, leaving it behind.)

"You told him I'd be back next week?"

"Yes. What's wrong with that?"

"But I've just been telling you —"

"Oh, you were upset. You didn't really mean all that."

"Of course I meant it." Tears of frustration were the hottest kind. "You don't believe what I say. You don't hear me."

"I do hear you. But I know better than you do what you mean."

If I had had a knife in my hand at that moment I would have plunged it in her heart. Or mine.

"You don't know everything, though," I said.

"Why? What's more to know?" She was slipping her apron over her head; in a moment she would begin cooking dinner in the clean broiler. Her bustling movements meant her patience with me was used up.

"I can't go back because I don't have the lens."

She stopped tying the apron and the strings fell gracelessly to her sides.

"What do you mean, you don't have the lens? Where is it?"

"I lost it."

"Lost it! When? Where? Why didn't you tell me?"

"Stop yelling. It's only a piece of plastic. It's not made of gold, you know."

"It may not be made of gold but it cost over a hundred dollars. Did you know that? Do you think we can throw hundred-dollar bills around? And all those visits? Did you think of that?"

I wished she would say exactly how much they paid for each visit to the eye doctor, but she just stood waiting, the air around her white-hot. I had never seen her this angry. I had flushed away all her hopes for my future life. I should have been one of the miscarriages.

"I've had about all I can take for one afternoon." She came very close to me, trembling. "Now tell me where you lost it so I can look for it."

"You can't look for it. It's gone. It's down the toilet."

She stared as if I had answered in another language. Very slowly, her face turned red, as something in her gathered and solidified. She was slow to anger, my mother was, even tolerant, but her vision had clear borders that couldn't be crossed. Once you crossed, there was no tolerance.

"You did it. You did it on purpose." As she stared, I had a powerful urge to laugh, as children laugh when they are so frightened and helpless there is nothing left to do — the broad absurdity of human life erupts in bubbles of hysteria. I bit my lips.

"How could you have done such a thing? I don't know what kind of child I raised. Tell me the truth. Why? Tell me, so I can know what kind of a person you are."

The truth again. She was obsessed with truth, as if by possessing it she would possess me. But if she knew the truth she wouldn't want me. I stared back and kept silent.

Her right hand shot out and slapped me hard on the cheek. The whole side of my face stung. My left hand ached to fly up and soothe the sting, but I willed it motionless. Only my head moved ever so slightly, as if to offer the other cheek.

I was almost sixteen and she had hit me. I would never speak to her again. The sting shot through me, a rash of shame and desire. I wanted the eye doctor. Instead of my mother standing before me, I wanted it to be him. I wanted to pull him in and feel him inside me. I was wet and furious. I closed my good eye and tried to conjure my mother into him, rearranging the cells, all the same carbon and nitrogen. I would have him right in the kitchen, right in her place. I wanted to spring on her, claw her and clasp her. But I didn't move.

"Now I'll have to call him again and tell him," she said. "After all that, to cancel. How do you suppose I'll feel doing that?"

"Forget it. I'll call." My final words to her, ever, I vowed.

"You'd better." She tied the apron strings and went to the sink to wash her hands. "And don't think you're getting another one," she flung over her shoulder. "You had your chance."

The days crept by, a denser phase of dread. I waited for my father's outburst when he found out. Did I think he was made of money? he would shout, forgetting I had never asked for the lens. But nothing happened; he remained his usual preoccupied self. Even worse, I dreaded calling the eye doctor to cancel the appointment and hearing the pleading, the madness. I knew that if for one moment I let myself truly hear his words, I would share his madness; I would be prey to love as I had been as a child. I too would dream of running away with him to some faraway place, as I had dreamed of running away with Bobby. And once we got to this place? I would have succeeded in leaving Brooklyn, but where else would I be?

He was tenacious — I knew that much about him. I could try leaving a message with his cheerful receptionist. But I knew that if I didn't appear on Monday he would telephone again. That mustn't happen. I would do what had to be done.

Seeing him would be safer than calling anyhow, for when I entered his office I became another person, an older person who didn't worry about the proper words for the occasion but remained true in her silence like those brave few who didn't answer the pig. Unwittingly he conferred this identity on me and I accepted it. I became the person he thought he was seeing, a person of mystery and power.

On Monday morning I washed my hair in the shower and let it hang loose around my face. I put on new hip-hugger panties and a black bra. Nylon stockings and pumps and a jersey dress. I hadn't planned to dress that way. I had planned to destroy his love, if that craziness could be called love, by appearing in the costume of a drab schoolgirl — pleated skirt, white blouse, knee socks, sneakers, hair held back by a rubber band. But at the last minute I couldn't do it. It wasn't for him, but for me, for the person I became in his office. She would not tolerate knee socks or an ugly pleated skirt. I stuffed make-up in my bag and ran downstairs.

The kitchen smelled of Cream of Wheat — flat, bland, and virtuous. My mother was at the stove, stirring. My father, waiting at the table with his newspaper, raised his head, looked me up and down approvingly, said good morning, and returned to the paper. So she still hadn't told him. Maybe there was a tacit alliance between us for which I should be grateful. I wasn't grateful. I would sooner endure his tantrums than accept her complicity. I had kept my vow of not speaking to her, except for the mechanics of daily life.

"I'll be home late. I'm going to study for a history test with a friend."

"Oh? What friend?"

I could make the friend a boy, an excellent distraction: she worried that I didn't go out with boys. Her notion of delicacy didn't permit her to express this outright — I might "feel bad"; rather, she reminisced about her own youth as an implicit example, presented as a wholesome, groupy whirlwind of parties and outings that suggested a Scott Fitzgerald story with all the sex and desperation leached out. That this ebullient social whirl had co-existed with the famous tribulations of immigrant life I found one of the great paradoxes of recent history, as if those gilded, gallivanting Daisys and Jasmines, Basils and Dexters, had turned up on the pages of the *Jewish Daily Forward*. But for all I knew such mixtures could occur, and my vision was simply too narrow to take them in.

If my friend were a boy there would be the inevitable queries: Who? Where does he live? Will his mother be home while you're studying? And afterwards: How was your afternoon? Coyly: Will I have a chance to meet him? No, I had no taste for lies so circumstantial.

"Arlene. You don't know her." It was the first name that occurred to me. Worse than Carlotta, Arlene was the girl who couldn't say no. She naturally had not been invited to pledge for a secret sorority and didn't seem to mind.

"Come home in time for supper, all right? I want to get things cleaned up early. We're having a card party. Don't you want to sit down and have some breakfast?"

"No, I'll get coffee on the way." I went over to kiss my father good-bye. He expected and liked this and it cost me nothing. Lately his indifference had made him lovable. He didn't force me to lie in order to be true to myself and what I now termed my private life. My father had no wish to partake of my, or for that matter anyone's, private life; that was hardly a man's vocation in Brooklyn, and perhaps not anywhere.

After the last class I went to the girls' room to apply my make-up, where I was joined by none other than Arlene. Side by side we stood before the cracked and clouded mirror, Arlene with an array of cosmetics spilling from her purse that humbled my tiny supply.

"This guy from Brooklyn College is picking me up," she told me. "A sophomore. He has a car."

"Oh really?" Boys in college bestowed a priceless status. "Where'd you meet him?"

"At some frat party." She pulled down the lower lid of her right eye and aimed a black pencil at it. "We're going to Coney Island."

"I thought everything there was closed up for the winter."

"It is. But we can still walk on the Boardwalk. What are you all dressed up for?"

"Oh, I have to see someone in Manhattan," I said airily.

Arlene was silenced. After she outlined the moist pink rim of each bottom lid, she held her right upper lid shut with one finger and, leaning forward over the sink till her face almost touched the mirror, drew a thick black line just above the lashes. She did this to the other lid and then, from the outer corner of each eye, drew a half-inch arc curving upwards. This was called doe eyes.

Watching her gave me grief. I couldn't wear eye-liner. The few times I had tried, at the bathroom mirror at home, I had botched the left lid because I couldn't see enough with my right eye. It didn't matter that I deplored the way Arlene looked, those thick lines giving her face a sickly, waif-like air, or that my father would have had a fit had I appeared one morning with doe eyes, the mark of trampy girls, or that eye-liner hadn't been feasible with the cumbersome contact lens. It was simply her freedom to do it, and the sure deliberateness of her hand holding the pencil. I grieved for all I could not do, for everything in the flesh that was arbitrary and unjust. The grief caught in my throat, and when I finally released a breath, acid anger filled my mouth. My mother should have complained when they brought me back to her imperfect. Even if it was too late, even if it meant facing down all her Brooklyn demons. For truth she should have made the gesture.

I finished much faster than Arlene. As I turned to leave she said, "Wait a minute. I'll walk out with you."

She wanted me to see her get into the college sophomore's car. She might offer me a ride to the subway, but I was in no hurry. What if I saw the porcelain-eyed man again?

"I can't, Arlene. I'm late already. Have fun on the Boardwalk."

"I will."

It was a long walk and I walked it slowly, as slowly as Susan of the sorority who never had to get anywhere urgently. The urgency was all on the eye doctor's side. A block from the station I slowed down even more, stopping to look at what was already killingly familiar — the plate glass windows of Dubrow's Cafeteria, where disheveled men huddled over cups of coffee; the giant neon ice cream sundae in the window of the Sugar Bowl, where boys plied their dates with malteds; the drugstore of pudgy Mr. Lieb and debonair Mr. Hoffner, whom my father called the Laurel and Hardy of the pharmaceutical world; the Carroll Theatre of my childhood Saturday afternoons; the new Chinese restaurant; the beauty parlor where Ella the beautician had cut my hair when I was thirteen and told me I was a beautiful girl, but she looked right into my eyes as she said it, so I was sure she only pitied me.

Displayed in the corner lingerie shop window were steely girdles and long-line bras of the sort my mother and presumably other settled women wore. These were so different from the wispy little things my friends and I wore that they might have been designed for another species altogether, and I hoped I would never become part of that species. Imagine the eye doctor undressing me and finding something like that!

I paused at the subway steps. I felt the man's fingers on me again and wanted to run the other way. Go on down, I commanded. But my legs were stone. Then my bad eye twitched impatiently and sent a message: How do I dare dream of escaping from Brooklyn and living in Paris if I can't even get on the subway to Manhattan?

The train was almost empty. Of course — not quite four o'clock, a dead hour. The trip home was the real danger. But that was far away. Maybe never. Something might happen, the eye doctor could carry me off . . . Maybe I had seen the last of Brooklyn.

I came up into dying winter light. It was beginning to snow, though it didn't feel cold enough — fine specks of snow like dust drifting in a weak beam of light, and the beam was everywhere, was the twilight itself. I walked past the church, past the doorman, into the elevator, lapsing into the passivity that draped me whenever I came near him. I sank into my body.

All was as I had left it three weeks ago: leather chairs, travel magazines, black and white prints of snowy scenes. The receptionist was gone. Waiting, reading a paper, was a white-haired man in a dark suit and tie with a briefcase at his feet. He must be a diplomat or a stockbroker, I thought, and in fact his paper was the *Wall Street Journal*. He glanced up and gave a vague smile. Clearly I had no effect on him. Whoever I became in the eye doctor's office, whatever the eye doctor saw, the stockbroker didn't see.

The office door opened; out came a mother holding a little girl by the hand. I couldn't see anything wrong with the girl's blue eyes. The doctor was startled to see me, I could tell, and I liked that. He only nodded, though, and motioned the stockbroker inside.

A new patient arrived, a large, heavily made-up woman in a fur coat and a hat with purple grapes on the brim. She took a long time getting out of her gear and settled down to chat about the weather, the unexpected early snow, in a juicy, operatic voice. I decided she must be an opera singer. It was odd to be talking to her about weather, its recent trends, its prospects. I had seen the weather but not felt it. For weeks I had been moving about in my private microclimate, over-heated, tropical. I was never cold.

The stockbroker soon emerged wearing a black eye patch over his left eye, which made him even more distinguished. As he slipped gracefully into his chesterfield I rose, but the eye doctor said, "Audrey, I think I may take Mrs. Gamanos first because she'll be just a few minutes. Would you mind?"

Before I could reply, the woman said, "Oh, but this young lady was here before me. I wouldn't want to —" She gazed at me appealingly.

"I don't think Audrey would mind. Is that all right, Audrey?"

How clever. I couldn't bring myself to say my mother wanted me home for supper so she could use my chair for the card party. "Yes, I guess so."

The lush lady was finished in less than ten minutes and he locked the outer door after her.

"Come inside." He locked that door too. "My God. I thought you might not come."

"I wasn't going to. My mother made me."

I didn't know where I ought to sit, or if I should sit at all. The big chair was for having my eyes examined and the couch was for the other thing. What exactly was I here for? The lens was what had brought me, and it no longer existed. The only other seat was the swivel chair at his desk.

"You look very nice. It's good to see you."

I shrugged.

"I know I frightened you last time. I'm sorry. I forgot how — how young you are. Do you know I went back to your records to see? I didn't realize. I figured, a high school senior . . . Not that it makes much difference . . . I don't mean to make excuses."

"I skipped."

"Yes. You would. Anyway, I said some things that must have sounded absurd. Even though they were true. Please, sit down at least." He waved at the couch and I sat.

"Look, Audrey, I've been very worried since we spoke on the phone. You're not . . . in any trouble, are you?"

"Trouble?"

"You know. You're not . . . ?"

"Oh! No, no." I could have laughed. Me, with a baby! I was barely more than a baby myself. Up in a closet I still kept an old doll with moving eyelids and auburn ringlets. Harriet was her name.

"You're absolutely sure?"

"Of course I'm sure," I snapped. I had had my period the week before, but I could no more say those reassuring words than I could fly. I blushed just thinking them in his presence.

"Jesus! I haven't slept all week. Your mother said you didn't feel well, you had to see the school nurse."

"That was just an excuse."

"I see." He sat down at his desk and spun the chair around a couple of times. "Well, it can happen, you know." He stared at me with a trace of malice. "You do know that's how it happens?"

I stared right back. "Now that you mention it, I guess I've heard that somewhere." He wouldn't weaken me by sarcasm. I had had plenty of training, in Brooklyn.

"You're not wearing the lens. Why?"

"I just didn't feel like it."

"Did it give you any pain or discomfort?"

"No," I said. "I was used to it by now."

He came and sat beside me on the couch. After a moment he put his arm around me and took my hand. "There's no hurry now. Stay a while. I know it's over, you don't have to explain." He gave an abrupt, sad little laugh. "Not that you would ever explain. But stay just this once." He put his hand on my breast.

I had no will. If my body stood up and left, well, all right. If it stayed on the couch, then that would happen. I wasn't involved. I never had been.

"Wait just a minute, Audrey, I've got to make a quick phone call."

As he dialed I studied the framed documents on the walls. He was a member of two ophthalmological societies. He had graduated from medical school in 1943, when I was four years old. On the ration lines. In love with Bobby.

"Hi," he said. "It's me. How's everything?"

If he was twenty-six when he graduated from medical school, he was thirty-seven now. Unless his schooling had been interrupted by the war — then I might be off by a few years. Had he been in the war? I wondered. Army, Navy, Air Force? Europe or Japan? He was younger than my father, anyway. That was a relief. My father was forty-three.

"Look, I've got an emergency here so I'm going to be late . . . I don't know, an accident. An hour or two. I'm sorry, sweetheart."

Was this being true to himself, or the opposite?

"I know, Helene, but what can I do?"

Helene. It wasn't a name bearing strong imagery, like Carlotta or Susan. There was a Helene at school, good in chemistry, short curly hair, very quiet. She had once helped me with an experiment in the lab. The eye doctor's name was Jeffrey, though I had never called him that. Helene and Jeffrey. Jeffrey and Helene. Jeff and Helene.

My breast tingled where he had touched it. The feeling was spreading through me in that uncanny way it had. I shifted around on the couch, crossing and uncrossing my legs. When would he get off the phone? For it seemed my body was not going to stand up and leave.

Idly, I shut my left eye to see how his desk looked as I decomposed it. An unfamiliar dark blob floated near one edge. I opened my good eye to see. It was a box labeled Eye Patches, For Medical Use Only. Yes, he had given one to the stock-broker; the lid of the box was still raised.

"Okay, tea bags," he was saying. "Aspirins, anything else?" At last he was beside me again.

"Helene." It came out. I hadn't planned it.

"Don't, Audrey."

He did everything very slowly, even more slowly than usual. No other patients were waiting. He moved his mouth all over my body for an endless time, and when finally he entered me and pushed his way deep inside, tears oozed down my face, as if I were already filled to the brim with myself and this extra bit of flesh made me spill over. But I knew I was crying because this would be the last time; it would be years before anyone touched me like this again, and even when they did, even if they were not awkward boys, it would never be exactly like this. It would never be him.

She was me, at that moment. She already knew what I know. This is so startling to come upon that I have to stop and contemplate it. And her. Oh yes, I see myself plainly, right there, bearing the seeds of all I would come to know.

He wanted to stay lying on top of me when it was over. He wanted to take the imprint of me on his body, he said, but I thought that even more, he wanted to leave his imprint on me. Soon we had to shift so I could bear his weight better.

"I want to ask you something," he said.

"What?" I hoped it was not what I had done with the lens.

"Who are you, really?"

"Oh, God," I groaned. I felt freer now that it was ending. I had never left anyone before; there was a melancholy thrill in it. "That's the kind of question they ask in a bad book."

"This isn't any book. I'm as real as you are."

I didn't know what the question meant or what form an answer might take. It sounded like a wrong step in a geometry proof, a step that could lead only to a dead end. I could have answered "What are you?" more easily than "Who?"

"Well," I said, "who do you want me to be?"

The ripples of his laugh slid from my shoulders down to my feet. "Either you're very wise or very ignorant. Which, Audrey?"

I knew which I thought it was, but I waited.

"I think it's very ignorant," he said, and he kept laughing as I pushed him off me.

"I meant it," I protested. "Does it really matter? You don't have to know who I am to feel the way you do. Maybe you'd feel different if you really knew."

"Maybe. But you don't like the way I feel anyway."

"I don't want to talk about it." I kissed his lips. "Now I want to ask you something." This was the most we had ever spoken. It made me feel extremely grown up. Pillow talk.

"Yes?"

I couldn't find the words. Those which sprang to mind seemed childish, almost as bad as his question. Are all men like you? Is this, what happened between us these months, a common thing, or is it extraordinary, and if it is, why did it happen to me? Is it so bizarre that I should be ashamed to appear on the street or enter my innocent little house and face my parents? Do you think men will like me, in this way? Or in a better way, knowing who I am? How can you like me, if you don't know me? It can't be only the way I look, can it?

"Do you have children?" I asked.

"Two boys."

"How old?"

"Ten and seven."

That was good. Much younger than I, and boys. I had nothing in common with them.

"Do you play cards?"

"Cards?" He looked puzzled. "No. Why?"

"I just wondered. What about your wife, what does she play?"

"Tennis, when she has the time."

"Tennis?"

"Yes, what's so odd about that?"

"Nothing, I just wasn't expecting it. I was thinking of . . . something more sedentary."

"She's not sedentary. She's a gym teacher."

I almost burst out laughing: gym teachers were intrinsically comical, with their military stance and barked commands, their ridiculous orange pinnies and green gym suits on square, muscular bodies, but I tamed my laugh to a polite smile of curiosity.

"Oh?"

"She's very athletic. She's a good skier."

A skier! Like the skiers in Movietone News, perhaps. Did she skim over the snow and leap in magnificent arcs, and maybe break bones and have them fixed by handsome doctors? That his wife was a skier brought my ancient fantasies thrillingly close.

"How did she get started skiing?"

"She just went, when she was in college, I think. She was also on the track team and played basketball. That probably doesn't mean much to you."

"Well, I'm not the athletic type."

"I know that."

"How do you know?"

"It's obvious. You don't have the body of an athlete, the muscle tone and so on. Oh, you're young and . . . and all that, but it's very clear."

Except for matters regarding my eye, this was the first time I had heard him speak of anything besides his feelings for me. The knowledge and cool objectivity pained me, suggesting the countless things he must know as a grown man. He could not be as obsessed as he pretended, if there were so many other things filling his head. The person I became in his office dimmed a little bit.

"Why, do you think I need to lose weight?"

"It has nothing to do with weight." He looked at my face and caught on. "No, I think you're perfect as you are, Audrey. Even a little too thin, in fact. Yes, maybe a little more here, and here —"

"Okay, okay."

"Now let me ask you something else," he said, "since you're so talkative today. Did you use the money to take that class you wanted, Scene . . . Scene something?"

"Scene Study. Not yet. It starts in two weeks. But I will."

"You've got it stashed away in a safe place? You're not going to spend it on candy or movies or whatever?"

"Of course not. Don't you believe me?"

"I do, I do. And what will you do in Scene Study?"

"Exactly what it says. We have to bring in something to present the first day. Everyone is planning the standard things, *Saint Joan, Member of the Wedding,* Juliet. I want to do something different. I'm looking through Eugene O'Neill. Do you have any suggestions?"

"I'm afraid not. I'm not a big reader. I haven't got the time."

"Oh, I knew that."

"How would you know?"

"It's obvious," I said. "You don't speak like a reader. Oh, you're intelligent and . . . and all that, but it's very clear."

For an instant his face was blank, then he smiled uncomfortably and feinted a punch to my jaw. "I think you have a great career ahead of you, Audrey."

I sat up. "Do you really think I could be an actress?"

"Probably. Though I wasn't thinking of acting."

I wasn't sure whether to be flattered or insulted. Either way, he wasn't taking me seriously. It was some sort of joke, more oblique than my father's customary taunts.

"Won't your parents wonder where you got the money for the class? What will you tell them?"

"They don't have to know everything I do. I'll say I'm going to the library."

"Ah. I guess I'm in no position to comment, am I?"

"I guess not. Oh, there's something I've always wanted to know. Why do they put those silver nitrate drops in newborn babies' eyes?"

"You're a girl of catholic interests, aren't you? That's to prevent blindness from gonorrhea. If the mother has gonorrhea the germs can get into the infant's eyes on the way out and cause blindness. The silver nitrate counteracts that."

"But not every mother has gonorrhea."

"Of course not. It's a preventive measure."

"I don't get it. Why don't they just test the mothers first instead of doing it to all the babies? There must be some test."

"Yes, but when do you administer it? Supposing she tests negative and then contracts it afterwards?"

"Well, say a month before. I doubt if any woman in her ninth month is going to find some total stranger to go to bed with and get gonorrhea."

"It's a matter of statistics, Audrey. There's no way of predicting what a woman will do, wouldn't you agree? This way is much more efficient. It's saved a lot of people. The incidence of infant blindness from gonorrhea is practically nonexistent."

"So it's done because they basically don't trust the women?"

"It's not a question of trust." He shifted around impatiently as though I were a recalcitrant student. "If there's a safe way to wipe out a serious danger, you do it. That's what medical progress is. You can't rely on probability, what individuals may or may not do."

"It doesn't make sense to me. Just because a handful of women may have it, you do it to all the babies. That's the opposite of efficient. It's like McCarthy, torturing everyone because maybe there's one person somewhere who's seriously thinking of overthrowing the government."

"My dear child, you're talking nonsense. There's no torture involved. It's the simplest of procedures. The baby doesn't feel it."

"How can you know what a baby feels? And how do you know it's so safe? Look at my eye. Maybe it wouldn't have happened."

"Aha! So that's what this is all about." He leaned over and gently stroked my eyelid with one finger. "Audrey, it's hardly possible that that could have caused the damage to your eye."

"My mother said the eye was fine when I was first born, and then after the drops, when she saw me, it was like this."

"Oh, you can't go by what a woman thinks she sees under those circumstances. I've never heard of anything like that happening."

"Well, maybe they poked it with the dropper, or broken glass from the bottle got in it, or something?" My questions, my persistence, surprised me. I hadn't known I was this interested.

He sat cross-legged, pondering. "It could have been anything. At this stage, and not having been there, I just don't know. I would tell you if I could. The eye is unusual, I will say that. I've never come across quite that cluster of symptoms."

"So I'll never know."

"I'm afraid not. But look, why worry over it? It obviously doesn't hinder your activities in any way. You've learned to compensate."

"What do you mean, learned to compensate?"

"I mean you can catch a ball, can't you? You can judge how far you'd have to walk to get to the telephone or the door. You can go down a flight of stairs without stepping off into space."

"And that's all compensation?"

"Partly, yes. You've learned through tactile experience, without binary vision."

"That's not so. I see what everyone else sees."

"I'm not saying you don't. But there's a process of combining left and right vision that you don't go through. You do it another way. It's hard to explain without getting technical. The point is, you're a beautiful, intelligent girl with your whole life ahead of you." He smiled and patted my hip. I almost cringed — the words were so beside the point. Pure Brooklyn. "And with the lens it doesn't show anyway. Right?" He might have been my mother.

"Mm-hm," I murmured, envisioning the lens afloat in the sewers of Brooklyn.

"So in effect you're perfect. Now give me a kiss and forget about it."

"Not now." I drew back.

"What's the matter? Do you think I'm very bad? I suppose you do."

"Why? I don't hold you responsible. You don't deliver babies anyway. You didn't start that stupid practice."

"Christ, Audrey, not that. There's no issue there. I mean bad in general. Because of what I've done. This. You."

What an idiot I was. "Oh. I don't know. I haven't thought a lot about it. Why, do you?"

"I not only think it, I know it."

"You're probably right. Isn't what you did called taking advantage of someone?"

"Oh, taking advantage. The first time, yes, that was a little crazy. You came back, though."

"I had to. The lens."

"Audrey, come now."

"I've been to so many doctors. It's a real drag, starting all over."

He grinned. "I won't let it go to my head, then."

I didn't understand that either. "If it's not taking advantage, then what do you feel so guilty about?"

"Interference. Disrupting your — what shall I say — innocent life. Don't you see? What it makes me out to be."

"But I didn't mind being disrupted —"

"Oh, I know. Don't I know it," he moaned. Rather wittily, I thought. "I've figured that out."

pleasure: being overpowered and weighed down, the warmth of him on my back and his breath on my shoulders, the sheer animal absurdity, the discomfort, the hard breathing, and his collapsing on me at the end — both of us collapsing like a house of cards, flat onto the leather couch, and his covering me from top to toe like someone shielding a child from enemy gunfire.

I turned over and he climbed on top of me and whispered my name. I thought I was ready — like the bride in the wine-colored book — but something was wrong. He seemed to be floundering around. When I realized what he was looking for my brain flipped over as my body had done. This was beyond inconceivable.

"No!" I twisted but he gripped me tight, one arm around my waist, and he was already there.

"Please, Audrey."

"No. Get away."

"I won't hurt you. I promise. You tell me if it hurts and I'll stop. Please," he whispered, and I felt a widening, and he was inside.

"Oh no," I said, but I wasn't struggling my hardest. I was getting interested. Horrible as this was, it was not boring, it was not Brooklyn. It might never happen again.

He pushed farther in and there was a slight searing, then a deep ache. Something dreadful was going to happen to my body, a splitting. Any minute.

"Stop, really."

He stopped. "Did I hurt you? I'm sorry." He reached around and began fingering me in front and my body started moving without my wanting to, little shudders. "Ah," he said.

I was moving with him, going somewhere I had not dreamed people could go, way beyond books. I was nothing anymore except the moving and knowing I would die of this or be punished for it. For there must be something truly wicked in me, to be always ready to be interested. He pushed farther in and it hurt again.

"No, stop!" I almost called out his name, but not quite.

He stopped and his hand stopped too. I was bereft. I gave a little cry.

"Well, what do you want, Audrey?"

Now that he was still, the pain was gone. The only pain was the absence of his hand touching me.

"Oh please," he whispered again. "Say do it."

He was lying to me. It was not a situation for "please." He could do whatever he wanted and he knew it.

"Just . . . just do . . ." The words wouldn't come out.

"No, Audrey." Not a tone you could say "please" in. A stern teacher, or my mother holding fast to her terms. "Not just for you. But I'll stop everything if you say so. Do you understand?"

He began moving again, slowly and carefully, and as his hand came back to me I gasped and burst into tears, and that was how it went. I couldn't tell if I was shaking from the sobs or from the pleasure, and after the choked noises in his throat and after he slipped out and fell beside me, I punched his couch, then turned around and punched him.

"What are you, some kind of pervert or something?"

He caught my wrists. "Do you really think so?"

"I don't know what I think. I don't know anything anymore." Hearing my words, I knew why he felt guilty.

"If you don't know by now . . . No, I'm not some kind of pervert. I just wanted to show you something." He held my wrists in one hand as if to show me, too, how useless was my flailing about. "That's what you wanted all along, isn't it? A thorough education?"

"I don't know what I wanted."

"I think I did my part pretty well, assuming you wanted to find out all about it. A little something off the beaten path."

"Oh, how can you say things like that! I didn't want anything! I didn't even want the goddamn lens."

"Well, I want something, dammit." He let go of my wrists. "I want you to remember me."

"Oh!" Something shifted in my head and I felt a settling of vision, as when a dizziness begins to pass. Or as if my eyes were seeing together, merging for the first time. What I saw was him. He was a person, like me. He wanted to be remembered, to have a place. All of a sudden I wanted to kiss him and say the kinds of words he said, but I couldn't, not after what he had done. "I would have remembered you anyway, without . . . that. But you also wanted to hurt me, didn't you?"

"No, I didn't intend to hurt you."

"I didn't say you *intended* to. I said you *wanted* to."

"Very fine distinctions for a little girl."

"Don't be patronizing."

"You're the patronizing one. You've always been. All right, maybe I did want to hurt you."

"But why?"

"Why do you think? You've hurt me."

"Me?" I rose up on my elbows to look down at him. "I haven't done a thing."

"You're exactly right. That's how you hurt." He stood up. "Let me have a look at the lens before you go."

"I don't have it with me."

"You don't?" He studied me for a moment, went to his desk, and reached under some papers. "You should have it checked from time to time. Your eyes are still changing. I'll give you the name of another doctor." He looked funny, leafing through his address book stark naked.

"Another doctor? Ha! Just what I need. No thanks, I think I'm very well used to it by now."

"As you like. You can tell your mother I said you don't need to come anymore, and don't forget to use the cleaning solution. You can get it at any drugstore. Call me if it ever starts to hurt. Or call someone."

"Could I have one of those?" I pointed to the box on his desk.

"What for? A souvenir?"

"I said I'd remember you. No, I just want one. You gave one to that man before me."

"Don't play games with your eyes, Audrey. You can do damage, fooling around."

"I won't. I'll use it for a costume or something. A pirate. It's a useful thing to have around the house."

He plucked an eye patch from the box, stretched the elastic, and flicked it over to me. It landed on my stomach. I ran my fingers over the black buckram and held the patch up to my good eye, then my bad. I was so intrigued by this new toy that I would have put it on right then, only I didn't want to hear him scold.

"Is it okay if I make a phone call?"

"Sure, go ahead." He was gathering his clothes. Suddenly he stopped. "Who are you calling?"

"My mother. To say I'll be late. You don't trust me, do you?"

"Not entirely. One word from you could destroy me."

"I'm not that kind of person."

I sat down in his swivel chair and picked up the phone. I had a plan. I was about to stage a scene, fantastical, born of too great a strain, too wide a sundering. I was going to talk to my mother in our ordinary Brooklyn way with the eye doctor close by, naked — the reverse of the telephone scene she had staged at home two weeks ago. He would be looking at me, maybe even touching me, while I told her I was finished studying with Arlene. In this way, at last I could bring my two worlds together, just as double vision, worlds side by side, can be corrected by a lens that fuses them. I was the one connection between the worlds; my voice humming over the wire would be the audible lens through which they merged. I needed this, even if only for a moment. And my mother, with her single vision, would never know what I had accomplished. She would never know the adventure of my life, in which I was giving her this vicarious role. Only the eye doctor would know.

But as I was dialing he went into the bathroom to dress. I suppose he did trust me to some extent, and he was no voyeur. My plans were ruined, everything stayed split. I heard the water running, and then my mother answered the phone.

"It's me. I'm leaving in a while. We had a lot to go over."

The eye doctor is washing, I was saying to her in another, secret voice. If my bad eye had had a voice it would have spoken these words. He's washing the traces of me off his . . . everything. He's rinsing out his mouth, rinsing me off his tongue and gums and the soft epithelial tissue inside his cheeks.

"Oh, Audrey, I was wondering what happened to you. We were just eating. I'll leave supper for you on a plate, 'cause I want to clean up. They'll be here in less than an hour."

"Okay. Don't worry, Arlene'll walk me to the subway."

I'm sitting in the eye doctor's chair with no clothes on. Oozing onto the chair . . . If you only knew . . .

"All right, 'bye. The studying go all right?"

"Fine." I can still feel him in me. Every opening. I'm very warm, Mom. Very.

I dressed quickly and wanted to rush out. It was over. I hated elaborate good-byes. But he took me in his arms and kissed me, stroked my face and hair and murmured words about not forgetting me. Just as in the movies. And I did my part gracefully enough, I thought.

My things were in the waiting room. He actually held my coat as I fumbled my way into it — I hadn't enough practice to do that with grace. It was painful to change, under his gaze, into a gawky schoolgirl, looping a scarf around my neck and hoisting a loaded book bag over my shoulder. I couldn't risk speaking — I was afraid I would cry, I felt so sorry for both of us, so cleaved and bleak, and my life evaporating before my eyes. How could I return to Brooklyn, where this didn't exist? But where else could I go?

Halfway down the hall I turned and waved. He was in the doorway, his hands raised and flat against the frame as if holding it up. His shirt was rumpled and his tie loose around his neck. He looked younger than he had ever looked, very young, almost of an age for me. I fled to the elevator.

The snow had stopped, leaving the sky velvety and clear, with frosty stars. Everything was lightly covered, and the sounds of cars and footsteps and doormen's whistles were all softened. I put the eye patch over my good eye. I would walk to the subway that way, half blind, with the white city shimmering hazily around me. The glowing globes of street lamps expanded and broke into starbursts, dazzling and blinding me with splinters of light. In between the lamps were impenetrable stretches of darkness — I couldn't see people approaching until they were nearly on top of me. I stretched out my arms for balance, the way we used to do playing Blindman's Buff at birthday parties. The church was a huge amorphous mass, its fine points and articulations lost in blur and darkness: a cave, not a haven. The headlights of cars were blinding too, bearing down on me like monster eyes; crossing the streets was madness. I needed to find my life, not lose it. I took off the eye patch and hurried to the subway.

I had forgotten to be afraid of the subway, and in fact there was little need for fear. Close to seven o'clock, rush hour was over. I found a seat, tugged *Anna Karenina* out of my book bag, and didn't look up until my stop, which I could feel by the length and rhythm of the ride, the intervals between the Brooklyn stations I no longer needed to count — they were imprinted on me like the stages of phylogeny are imprinted on the embryo: Clark, Borough Hall, Hoyt, Nevins, Atlantic, Bergen, Grand Army Plaza, Brooklyn Museum, Franklin, Nostrand, Kingston, Utica.

It was snowing again. I put the patch over my bad eye and saw clearly the usual sights: the central mall and wooden benches of Eastern Parkway, the neon sign of Dubrow's Cafeteria lit red for evening and the lonely men still huddled over their coffee, the lingerie shop, the newsstand, all with the patina of tenderness snow gives the world. Just what I would have seen with both eyes. My bad eye's talents weren't needed here.

I switched the patch. A test. Could my bad eye get me home? Was it of any practical use, or were its talents good for nothing but adventure and trouble?

Not much of a test. I knew Utica Avenue so well I could have walked it blindfolded. The Sugar Bowl, where people from school might be sipping ice cream sodas as I passed; Laurel and Hardy's drugstore; the lighted marquee of the Carroll Theatre announcing, through the falling snow, this week's movie. I couldn't read the title, but whatever it was, I was sure the characters kissed and parted, kissed and parted.

Traffic was sparse. In the deep distance, splatters of red and green alternated on wavy poles. I crossed easily and turned down Montgomery Street, where one building had a short cut to East New York Avenue, useful on cold days. You took the elevator to the basement, went through a dimly lit corridor past the boiler and piles of garbage, and emerged in the back of the candy store, saving a block. But no, it was too dark and deserted for that corridor. I chose the long way, outdoors.

Suddenly there in the snow, only minutes away from home, a feeling of limitless buoyancy flowed through me like breath. It seemed I might leave the earth and sail up unimpeded, as the snow around me was sailing down, and float right over Brooklyn up to where the stars drifted — I couldn't see them but they were there. I didn't want to float away, though; I was so enraptured that I wanted to remain here on earth, or maybe just a few inches above, and dance. Everything seemed perfect and right; the world, glistening and abundant, unfurled its rightness and perfection — how come I hadn't noticed before? Of course I would have everything I wanted, my life would be all I dreamed. And even if it weren't, it didn't matter; nothing that could happen mattered; it was enough to be alive on this moist and spinning globe. Every flake of snow tingled on my skin, joyously cold and hot at once. There was not even any more death in this miracle of a world, just wave after wave of life and motion. This was too good to be true, I knew. I had been touched by something beyond the palpable. It came from nothing that had happened to me today or ever, beyond circumstance, out of nowhere, a gift that wouldn't last, but I wanted it to last as long as such gifts could. I wanted to prolong it and also to let it be, not touch it for fear of shattering it. I didn't even stop walking. No change must break the enchantment. It would end any second, but I would remember and hold it, an intimation of what might be, and because it was so beautiful I knew remembering it would be heartbreaking.

It lasted longer than I had dared hope, so long that I was dazed with gratitude, and then it started slowly to dissolve, and when I neared the corner and saw the figure of a man approaching, it vanished abruptly as though it never was.

I switched the patch to my right eye so that I could see. He wore a pea coat and wool scarf, and was tall and broad-shouldered. His hands were dug into his pockets as he lumbered along with his head down, a man lost in himself. About thirty feet away, he looked up, noticed me, and slowed down. His mouth opened slightly. He raised a hand and my stomach bounced. Then settled. Bobby! If he hadn't come along I might still be in bliss.

"Audrey! Long time no see. What happened to your eye? Did you have an accident?"

I pulled off the patch and stuffed it in my coat pocket. "No, I'm fine. A doctor gave it to me for eye exercises. Didn't you ever notice something wrong with my right eye?"

"No." He kept grinning and rubbing his gloved hands together. "Maybe I should've looked harder. So how've you been? I don't see you in the store much these days."

"No. Busy, you know. School and all."

I asked after his wife, Bobby, and the baby. Wondrously, I remembered his name — Donny. I had seen him crawling around the store last summer, making little mountains out of sawdust. He was a handful, Bobby replied, and Bobby was pregnant again.

"It would be nice to have a girl this time. You know," he said wistfully, "someone to sit quietly on her daddy's lap. Donny is never still for a minute."

"Even girls don't sit very long," I said, and we stomped our feet in the snow.

"You certainly are looking great, Audrey. You've grown up."

"These things happen."

"An answer for everything. Same old Audrey."

"Well, I think I'd better go on home. Good seeing you."

"Listen, what do you say to a cup of coffee somewhere first? Talk about old times, catch up. Maybe you can give me some advice."

"About what?"

"Oh, I don't know. I'm thinking of getting a job. This working for my father is a dead end. I don't want to sell chickens all my life. And Bobby's not the type who'll want to do what my mother does. Come on. You'll warm up."

"I wish I could, Bobby, but my mother's expecting me and I'm late already. They're having a card party."

"So give her a call."

"What are you thinking of, the Sugar Bowl?"

"Nah, it's filled with all those kids. I'll take you to the Blue Feather."

That was a local bar whose dark windows displayed a blue neon feather. No one I knew had ever crossed its murky threshold. It was a joke around school: What sorts of primitives frequented the Blue Feather and what unknown caverns of Brooklyn could they come from?

"Oh no, I think I'd better not. Thanks anyway."

"Some other time, then. Let me walk you home, at least."

Bobby sounded even less like a book than the eye doctor at his worst. I had read many novels of unrequited love at long last rewarded, of joys arriving too late. The women in the novels were always brimming with exaltation or regret, but I felt nothing.

"Did you really never notice my eye?"

"No. But I'm not very observant. Let's see." I faced him and opened wide. "I can't see anything wrong."

"It's probably too dark," I said.

"Well, nobody's perfect. I grew up with my mother, so little things don't bother me. You hardly notice if you really care about someone. So do you have anyone good at school? Is Memling still doing American History? He used to sing 'The Battle Hymn of the Republic' when he got to the Civil War. Every single stanza."

"They retired him last year. He must've gone out singing. I managed to get Carlino. You know, Pre-Marriage for Senior Girls? I was on the waiting list and then they opened another section by popular demand."

We were at East New York Avenue, a huge two-way thoroughfare with no traffic lights and a stream of whizzing cars, even in the snow. Bobby grabbed my elbow — "Come on! Now!" — and we raced across during a short lull. Only half a block to my house.

"You girls are the lucky ones. All we ever had was Hygiene. You know what they told us? Fellas, you have five thousand shots in you. Don't waste them."

I must have looked startled, for he quickly added, "Oh, excuse me, Audrey. That just slipped out."

"It's okay. I can take it." I almost countered with Mrs. Carlino's definition of Petting, still in my book bag where it had lain all day, through classes and Arlene's eye make-up and the subway and the doctor, but I knew enough not to.

"So how old are you now? Around eighteen?"

"I'll be sixteen in two months." We paused at the snow-covered steps in front of my house. Tomorrow my father or I would have to shovel. Not enough to have school closed, though, unless it kept up all night.

"No kidding? You could have fooled me. Jailbait." He

chuckled and tweaked my nose. "A pretty girl, out on these dark streets so late . . ."

"Oh, come on, Bobby." I frowned. "I'm going in."

He raised his hand the way my father did, to ward off assault. "Jeez, I keep putting my foot in my mouth, don't I? No offense. Listen, I remember when you were in kindergarten and came into the store holding your mother's hand. You were a cute kid. My mother liked you too, the way you used to watch her do the chickens."

"Oh, I loved to watch her. And I had such a crush on you, it was pathetic. Did you know?"

"Really? Me? But you were just a baby. Oh, wait a minute, I remember you wrote me a letter when I joined the Navy. It was a cute letter."

"I missed you. Then you came back and got married. You threw me over without mercy. Well, that's life, isn't it?"

"Sure is," he agreed.

"What did you do in the Navy, anyway?"

"I was a seaman. Deck force. We kept up the ship, painting and repairs and so on. We were stationed in Hawaii most of the time. Great place for swimming."

I started up the steps. "Bobby, why don't you try looking for a job in the city? There's so much happening there. I go in a lot because of the eye doctor. It's another world, really."

"And travel forty minutes each way on that crowded subway? Nah, who needs that?"

"Well, thanks for walking me home."

"Any time. And listen, Audrey, I didn't mean anything, you know that."

"I know. 'Night, Bobby."

From the porch I watched him recede, hands in his pockets again, head down. Under the streetlight his silhouette was haloed in snow and his profile took on a bluish cast. The crystals on his pea coat gleamed like rhinestones.

I hadn't needed my good eye to get home. I could do it without eyes. Or someone like Bobby would come along and willingly take me. On that dreamy one-eyed walk from the subway, the familiar streets and shops had barely existed; my entire past barely existed, could be rolled up into a mote in the eye and winked away. As I stood on my porch, just outside the arc of warm light from within, already hearing the rumbly voices of the men, and beneath them, in counterpoint, the lithe, fluty voices of the women, I was sure my true life had not yet begun. And when it did, oh how freely I would float.

I opened the door and stepped into the card party, in full swing.

There they were, my father, Mr. Zelevansky, Mr. Ribowitz, Mr. Singer, Mr. Capaleggio, and Mr. Tessler, amidst their cards and glasses of soda and ashtrays and nuts and pretzels. I could greet them easily now. They were men like the eye doctor. They took off their glasses and their clothes in the same way, and climbed on their women. And though I could readily picture them doing that, climbing on their women — busy at mah jongg in the next room — I could not so readily imagine their making love to them, cupping a breast in one hand and leaning over till the tongue found the tip of the nipple, or tracing the line of the torso with a tender thumbnail. If they did, it was beyond my vision.

I beamed a smile on all and yanked off my scarf. My father's back was to me. I bent to kiss him on the cheek and he accepted my kiss with a slight turn of the head, his eyes detaching reluctantly from his cards. "Oh, cold, Audrey!"

"It's snowing again," I sang out in the juicy operatic tone of Mrs. Gamanos in the doctor's waiting room. "Hello, Mr. Tessler. Hi, Mr. Cappy. Hello, hello. How are all you gentlemen?" As I circled the table I let my hand alight for a second on Lou Zelevansky's shoulder. "Hi, Lou, how are you?" He, after all, was the one I had known since my birth, the one with whom my parents had listened to Joe Louis knock out Max Schmeling in the first round before I was conceived.

I expected the men might drop their cards in shock and my father leap from his chair, demanding to know what I thought I was doing, addressing Mr. Zelevansky by his first name. Or he would burst out laughing and say, "Look who's grown up all of a sudden! Who does she think she is?" But nothing happened. No one seemed to notice. It was easier than I had thought, just as what I had done with the eye doctor was easy. There for the taking, as perhaps many of life's privileges were. That crucial secret must be what distinguished the adventurous from the timid. Mr. Zelevansky replied that he was fine, thank you, and inquired in kind, and the game continued.

I proceeded through the archway to the dining room, where I could hardly say hello before the smiling women were exclaiming over me — how suddenly grown up, how was I doing in school, wasn't I cold, wasn't I hungry?

Not cold, never cold, but hungry. A plate was waiting in the oven: roast chicken — maybe Bobby had delivered it while I lay on the eye doctor's couch — rice and string beans. Applesauce for dessert, my mother called into the kitchen, but if I could wait till later they would be having apple pie.

"Poor Audrey, she has to stand while she's eating. We've taken her chair," said blond, garrulous Mrs. Tessler. "Here, dear, use my chair. I don't need it — I'm East this hand."

"Thanks, it's quite all right. I don't mind standing." I was perfectly comfortable leaning on the doorframe, observing the games and gnawing on my chicken leg. In my head, I was matching the women with their husbands, imagining them doing what I had done. Mr. Cappy in the distance, slender and ruddy, his pipe protruding from his mouth at an interesting angle, was the only one of the men besides my father who might by prevailing movie and advertising standards be called attractive. I envisioned him curved over Mrs. Cappy, a hollow-cheeked woman with glinting black eyes, fuzzy hair, long gold earrings, and jutting bones. Her eyes closed, her earrings quivered. Roly-poly Mrs. Tessler straddled her roly-poly husband — a man so quiet that for a long time I had assumed he must have a cleft palate like the chicken flicker — on one of the king-sized beds from their furniture store, the pair of them bouncing like green-eyed teddy bears. Mr. Tessler and Mr. Singer, the possible widower or divorcé, were known to be inseparable friends as well as business partners; perhaps Mr. Singer watched.

Had these women, hair carved by beauticians, bodies encased in God knows what steely underclothes, ever felt what I felt? Was it possible? If they had, how could they be sitting here calmly playing mah jongg?

I closed my good eye, and my bad eye, serene and shameless, conjured up the bunch of them frolicking around the living room, a welter of pink and tan flesh tripping over the furniture, moans and leers and giggles. From far away I heard Mrs. Tessler ask what I was taking in school. I blinked and refocused, and the orgy vanished. Pre-Marriage, I replied. We would be doing budgets soon, and bathing a rubber doll in a plastic tub.

"I'm surprised they waste your time like that. You'd be better off doing English or history or something. There's plenty of time later on to learn how to bathe a baby."

I had misjudged her. "That's true," I agreed, "but it's an easy course, you know, and they let you take it easy senior year when most of the requirements are over."

"Hm. Seems to be rushing things, especially if you're going to college. So where do you think you'll go, Audrey? Brooklyn? Or City?"

"I haven't decided, I've been so busy. I have another month or so to apply. I wish I could go out of town."

"Out of town," echoed my father, wandering in to commence his customary teasing of the women. He would examine their tiles and ask foolish questions, pretending to be at once too simple-minded and too lofty to understand their game, and then threaten to reveal their strategies to the others. They would scold and he would revel in their scolding.

"Out of town. I'd have to be made of money to do that. Anyway, this one doesn't have the sense to come in out of the rain, how can she go out of town?"

"I just came in out of the snow, didn't I?" I managed to find my way home from Manhattan, I started to say, but caught my tongue in time.

I backed into the kitchen, kicked up the doorstop, and let the swinging door fly. My cheeks and eyeballs were burning. Was that for calling Mr. Zelevansky Lou? No, he would have attacked that on the spot. He must know about the lens. But how could he? He hadn't this morning, and my mother was far too shrewd to break the news right before a card party. He had barely looked at me when I entered, and in any case was no more observant than Bobby. Probably his partner had made a stupid move and he was losing. Why even seek a cause? Since when did his spasms of bitterness require provocation? It meant nothing to him that I had broken the bank — I was still not smart enough to take care of myself. I wished I could hurl in his face all that I knew now, make him see it and wince and burn as I did.

"Why must you say things like that?" I heard my mother scold. "What did she do?"

"What did I say? Only the truth. Now, what have we here? Why do you have those green ones all mixed up with the red? Shouldn't they be separate?"

"Oh, go back to your men. We were doing fine before you came to pester us."

I was trapped in the kitchen — I couldn't get upstairs without passing him, and I couldn't bear to be near him. His words thudded in my head. I leaned against the sink, trying to drive them out by concentration. The eye doctor. I could get wet just remembering. I was absorbed in how far my concentration might take me, when the kitchen door swung open. My mother must be East, with about ten minutes to spare.

She took raw vegetables out of the refrigerator and heaped

them on the table. When they were all arrayed like a still life, she drew a deep breath and faced me. "Don't feel so bad. Don't take him seriously. You know he doesn't mean any harm."

"What does he mean, then?"

"He just does it to show off."

"But what is he showing off?"

"Audrey, you can't go around analyzing every little thing so deeply. Where will it get you? Just forget it. Here, as long as you're standing around, cut these tomatoes into quarters." She handed me a knife.

"I really wish I could get my own apartment."

"Someday you will, I'm sure." Hastily, she arranged slices of green pepper and radishes in an artistic design, grabbing the tomato quarters as fast as I could cut them.

"I'm not talking about someday. If I have to go to college in the city, maybe I can find a cheap place and get a part-time job to pay for it."

"I can't pay attention to one of your speeches right now, Audrey. Can't you see I'm trying to do something?"

"I'm not stopping you. I'm helping you. This is my future I'm talking about. It's also possible not to go to college right away, you know. I could move out and get a job in the city and save up to go later. At night, if necessary."

She was attacking the peel of a cucumber in quick, tense strokes. Into her silence came the sweet, burbling sound of the mah jongg tiles; their swift rhythms meant the hand must be nearly over. Any moment she would be called back to the game. Her knuckles on the fist clutching the peeler were white. "I don't know what's gotten into you. I'm sorry your father made that remark. It certainly was not called for. But you don't have to blow it up all out of proportion —"

"I'm not. I could get a decent job. I know how to do a lot of things. Did it ever occur to you that I might like a change of scene? Or some privacy at this point? Maybe you would too."

"Privacy! What kind of privacy does a girl your age need, I'd like to know? You have a bedroom with a door. Isn't that enough?"

She wasn't shrieking as I had shrieked in my scene with Lizzie weeks ago (there was the card party; anyway she was not a shrieker) and her words were not a literal replication of my own. Still, I felt an ecstasy of triumph. I had re-created my improvisation. Life was imitating art.

They were calling her name from behind the closed door. "The hand is over. We're starting." I heard the scrambling of tiles and imagined the mass of fingers, decked with engagement-ring diamonds and gold bands, circling over the center of the table with the potent movements witches make over their brew.

"I have to go now. But I don't want to hear any more of this nonsense about jobs and apartments. I'm surprised at you. I thought you had a pretty good home here. I feel very bad. What do you think we've struggled for all these years? Instead of appreciating it you can't wait to get away. I'm coming in a minute," she called to the women. "And if you're going to keep hiding in here you might as well slice some bagels and arrange the lox on the white platter." With that she wiped her hands on a dish towel and rushed at the door, pushing so hard that it swung back and forth several times after her, in arcs of diminishing range and speed and urgency, until finally it settled.

Invading my triumph was a queasiness — something not quite fair, not quite true about the scene. Bad faith was what the acting teacher, who had existentialist leanings, would no doubt call it, since my mother was not aware of the predetermined script. He told us bad faith always brought a queasy feeling, like having your cake and eating it and feeling faintly nauseated by it.

Well, so what? Hadn't she always acted in bad faith too, from not protesting about my eye, to using the lens to pay for her negligence (making me pay!), to abandoning me to the hands of the eye doctor? Even my father's outright insults were preferable. Crude, cruel, but honest.

No, that was worse faith. Everyone knew girls favored their fathers, and the reasons did not bear close scrutiny. Not just now, anyway.

I cut the bagels and arranged the lox on the platter, thinking of jobs I might get. Restaurant work, assisting the chef. A clerk, a salesgirl. But I knew these tepid fantasies were as false as the scene we had played. My part was prescribed as surely as my mother's, for as long as I remained in Brooklyn. Next year would find me right here, going to a local college. And I should be grateful for that, she would point out: after all, she hadn't had the same opportunity. And according to her script she was right.

My lines in class had been uncannily prophetic, and I could take some pride in that. Yet the more I thought about it, the more queasy I grew. Was it my script or hers? Who was reading from whose?

Two hours later, as I lay on my bed aswirl in the torments of poor Anna Karenina, my mother called up the stairs, "Audrey, we're having a snack. Do you want to come down and join us?"

The cards and mah jongg tiles and bridge tables were gone. The dining room table was open to its full length, laden with food, and around it was assembled the card party, husbands next to wives. I took a seat far from my parents, between Lou Zelevansky and Mrs. Ribowitz, whom my father privately called the intellectual because she taught calculus at a high school, attended lectures at the Ethical Culture Society, and spoke in what he called a teacher's voice. Though I defended Mrs. Ribowitz on principle when my father mocked her, there was indeed an asperity to her chalky face and thin hair; I couldn't readily see her panting under Mr. Ribowitz, his great electric bulb of a head bent over her face. Mrs. Ribowitz illustrated a subtlety I came to understand only long afterwards: no woman in Brooklyn was barred from the life of the mind. She could choose the life of the mind or the life of the body, but she could not have both. If she chose the former, it was considered that she had done so by default. And, given Brooklyn, perhaps she had.

"I always predicted this would happen. It was only a matter of time," my father was saying. "I hope it's on television too. Let's see him have a taste of what he rammed down people's throats."

The pig. I wrenched my mind from Anna's trials and listened expectantly.

"Poetic justice," murmured Mrs. Ribowitz. "Like a Shakespearean tragedy."

"Tragedy my foot," said yellowish Mr. Singer, spreading cream cheese on a bagel. "The guy's just a goddamn SOB. They should have done it long ago."

"Everything in its time," said Mr. Capaleggio.

"That may be," said Mr. Ribowitz, "but it's too late for some people. My brother-in-law's sister's father-in-law, that's my sister Essie's husband's family, was called down, and this fellow really was a pinko, a union organizer. A man close to seventy, so humiliated he came home and had a stroke and now he's in a wheelchair, drooling. Finished off. The family is in a state of shock. And such fine people. Whatever their views. Very fine. They loaned Essie's husband money to put the boys through school and Essie doesn't have it to pay back yet and she feels terrible. Her boys are working two jobs to pay them back. We even gave her something to give them."

"Tsk, tsk," said everyone.

I could not believe this. "Where does he live?" I asked.

"Oh, over on Cortelyou Road, near Rogers. He's lucky he owns his own home, because they might have thrown him out of an apartment."

This was in the very heart of Brooklyn. I knew the corner.

"Never mind that," said Mrs. Tessler. "Our friend Irv Krasnow got the business a year ago on that loyalty oath. Utterly destroyed."

"Who is he?" asked my mother.

"Oh, Pauly and I knew him way back in high school. He always had, you know, progressive ideas. He married my cousin Charlotte's husband's sister. You met him at Flo's wedding, don't you remember? A professor at Hunter College? Anyway, he refused to sign a piece of paper, just on principle, he says he has nothing to hide and I believe it, but who knows and anyway what difference does it make now? He lost his job, they borrowed from everyone, and now he's selling shoes on Flatbush Avenue. His hair turned white. His children are so aggravated, you can't imagine. His son didn't even get into med school, and he had the highest grades in his class."

"Where do they live?" I asked.

"What?" She shot me a curious look. "Where they live? They live over in Sheepshead Bay. Ocean Avenue somewhere."

This too, Brooklyn. I had ambled around there last spring with slow-walking Susan, who wanted a glimpse of a certain boy's house. It was a fishing neighborhood. Whole families stood on the piers at the bay on Sunday morning dangling their lines in the water, then dumped the fish into buckets at their feet. We had found the house, finally, with a gray De Soto parked in the driveway.

"Look," said Belle Zelevansky, "everybody has someone. Our Carol's piano teacher's brother, the sweetest man you could ever hope to meet. We see him every year at the recitals — they're a musical family. He used to play in the orchestras for the Broadway shows, but the union put him on a blacklist and he can't get work anywhere. He taught violin at a school downtown, but he lost that job too. A man with four young children."

"Where does he live?"

"What is this where-they-live business, Audrey?" Lou Zelevansky poked me in the shoulder. "What are you, working for the FBI or something?"

"Sorry. I was just curious."

"That's all right," said Belle. "I don't mind. They live not far from here, as a matter of fact. On Union near Nostrand. But if things don't get better they'll have to move in with Carol's piano teacher. She has a two-family house. She'll just have to ask the tenants to move."

Nostrand. One of the stations on my subway ride from the eye doctor's. Only two away from ours, Utica. I had passed it twice this afternoon while I was supposedly studying with Arlene, an afternoon that felt very distant. Here was reality — these many victims, the clash of ideologies, politics somersaulting personal destinies. Movietone News in the making, previewed around our dining room table.

"This could never have happened under Roosevelt," said my mother.

"Oh, you and your Roosevelt," my father grumbled. "That is a moronic remark for two reasons. First of all under Roosevelt they were our allies. We needed them to fight the war. So of course it couldn't have happened. Second of all, do you realize he knew all about the camps? They all knew, Churchill, de Gaulle. It was no secret. They just didn't care enough to do anything, that's all."

"I can't believe that," said my mother. "Where did you hear that?"

"It's true," said Mrs. Ribowitz. "Things are coming out. You read bits and pieces in magazines and put it together. We could have taken refugees in the beginning but we didn't."

"You see?" sneered my father, with a nod of esteem for the intellectual. "Millions of people rotted away and your Roosevelt didn't lift a finger till it was too late, and even then he waited till he couldn't help himself."

"First of all he's not *my* Roosevelt, and second of all we don't have to discuss these things while we're eating."

"I'm through eating," said my father, pushing his plate away. "Is there any more coffee?"

My mother fetched the coffee pot and poured seconds while they all argued about Roosevelt.

"Well, whatever you say, I frankly find that very hard to believe," she said. "I would have to read that with my own eyes. Do you know, I was so upset the day he died I almost started a fire in the oven."

"You didn't almost start it," corrected my father. "You started it. It almost spread when you got the bright idea of pouring water over it."

"All right, pardon me. The fact remains. That's how I felt."

"I never thought he was the saint he was cracked up to be," said Mr. Capaleggio. "I always had my suspicions."

"Oh, you're a fine one to talk," said my father. "Your Duce didn't exactly help matters, did he?"

"How dare you talk to him like that!" said Mrs. Cappy, half rising out of her chair. "He was born right here in Brooklyn. He's as much an American as you are, if not more. He's never even crossed the ocean. And both his younger brothers fought in the war, and Vincent came home with his foot blown off and a Purple Heart."

"Yeah, take it easy, fella," said Lou Zelevansky to my father. "You're way out of line there. Calm down and drink your coffee."

Mr. Cappy just puffed on his pipe. "Leave him alone. I know what he's like. He doesn't mean it."

"Okay. Okay. I spoke out of turn. No harm done, all right?"

I was stunned. My father, apologizing man-to-man. I wouldn't have thought him capable of it.

"But I'll tell you one thing," he continued, his voice low but still itching. "It is your Pope. That is the case, isn't it? And you can't tell me he didn't look the other way for years."

"He's not my personal Pope. He's the Pope, that's all. What do you expect me to do about it? Challenge the Vatican? Start a vendetta on behalf of my Jewish friends?"

"Don't you think we should change the subject?" said Mr.

Tessler, who so seldom spoke that his damp throaty voice was always a surprise. "I'm sure we could find a more congenial topic."

"That's an excellent idea, Nat. In a minute you can all tell me what you think of my apple pie."

This was my cue to leave. I could not bear a congenial topic after discovering there was life in Brooklyn. Passion. Conflict. Thought. An ample scene for both my eyes. But only under cover of darkness, with the children safely unconscious.

"Excuse me, I'm going up to bed. This has been extremely interesting."

"Yes, you really got an earful tonight, didn't you, Audrey?" said Lou Zelevansky, giving me one more avuncular poke, in the ribs.

"Oh, cut it out, Lou," I said. "I'll be black and blue in the morning."

My mother gasped and her mouth stayed open to reprimand me, but she thought better of it. "Don't you want to wait for dessert?"

"No thanks, I've had enough. Good night. Good seeing you all." I started for the stairs.

"Did you hear the one about Sister Kenny and FDR?" said Lou. "Sister Kenny was helping him into the pool one day when —"

"Could you hold it just a minute?" my mother interrupted, and there was a heavy silence.

When I reached the top of the stairs I called down, "It's okay, I'm not listening." I shut the door of my room. A moment later I heard a burst of collective laughter.

With the money the eye doctor gave me I took the class in Scene Study. The passage I brought in the first day was from *A Streetcar Named Desire.* I was Blanche DuBois, welcoming the adolescent newsboy into her sister's living room. The acting teacher, the same spindly teacher, recruited a boy to play opposite me. He hadn't very much to do in the scene, merely light Blanche's imaginary cigarette and receive her attentions, though who can tell what fertile residue these left in his life — he is only an incidental character and one needn't worry about him. " 'Young man,' " I said. " 'Young, young, young man. Has anyone ever told you that you look like a young Prince out of the Arabian Nights?' " I crooned in a sultry voice, and as he stood in agonies of awkwardness I reached out to stroke not his cheek but the air a half inch from it, which I thought was a brilliant touch. The air near his cheek was unusually warm, and his eyes looked terrified, yet at the same time ever so faintly amused. The next lines called for me to kiss him, but I didn't. " 'Now run along, now, quickly! It would be nice to keep you, but I've got to be good — and keep my hands off children.' " The class was awestruck.

It was never again as it had been with the eye doctor. I was right, at fifteen, when I foresaw that. Not only because he was the first; not only because he was . . . he was . . . Oh, yes, because he was the first, and himself, he was something that flies off the page every time I capture a word to define it. But also because never again could there be that particular set of voluptuous, atavistic, outrageous, and above all delicate circumstances.

I left Brooklyn. I leave still, every moment. For no matter how much I leave, it doesn't leave me.

I didn't become an actress in the end, but instead this I who makes up stories. In this story, I can't help wondering if I have succumbed to the temptation of any maker of a memoir — to present it more dramatically, improve the events so that they yield a more precious truth.

> How completely and
> how deeply faithless we are,

writes the poet Marina Tsvetayeva,

which is
to say: how true we are to ourselves.

Perhaps I haven't succeeded in finding the girl I was, but only in fabricating the girl I might have been, would have liked to be, looking backwards from the woman I have become. For now I could do easily all that she did with such effort, though now it couldn't happen. The very notion is an Escher construction: I am not a sheltered child but a grown-up version of a child who never was. And maybe I am this way because she never was, couldn't be. And yet it feels so real. If it wasn't a memory to begin with, it has become one now.

Does being true to one's self mean offering the literal truth or the truth that should have been, the truth of the image of one's self? It hardly matters by this time. By this time the border between seeing straight on and seeing round the corners of solid objects, between the world as smooth and coherent and the world as dissociated skinless particles, is thoroughly blurred. No longer a case of double vision, but of two separate eyes whose separate visions — what happened and what might have happened — come together in what we call the past, which we see with hindsight.

Memory is revision. I have just destroyed another piece of my past, to tell a story.

FOR THE BEST IN PAPERBACKS, LOOK FOR THE

In every corner of the world, on every subject under the sun, Penguin represents quality and variety—the very best in publishing today.

For complete information about books available from Penguin—including Pelicans, Puffins, Peregrines, and Penguin Classics—and how to order them, write to us at the appropriate address below. Please note that for copyright reasons the selection of books varies from country to country.

In the United Kingdom: For a complete list of books available from Penguin in the U.K., please write to *Dept E.P., Penguin Books Ltd, Harmondsworth, Middlesex, UB7 0DA*.

In the United States: For a complete list of books available from Penguin in the U.S., please write to *Dept BA, Penguin*, Box 120, Bergenfield, New Jersey 07621-0120.

In Canada: For a complete list of books available from Penguin in Canada, please write to *Penguin Books Ltd, 2801 John Street, Markham, Ontario L3R 1B4*.

In Australia: For a complete list of books available from Penguin in Australia, please write to the *Marketing Department, Penguin Books Ltd, P.O. Box 257, Ringwood, Victoria 3134*.

In New Zealand: For a complete list of books available from Penguin in New Zealand, please write to the *Marketing Department, Penguin Books (NZ) Ltd, Private Bag, Takapuna, Auckland 9*.

In India: For a complete list of books available from Penguin, please write to *Penguin Overseas Ltd, 706 Eros Apartments, 56 Nehru Place, New Delhi, 110019*.

In Holland: For a complete list of books available from Penguin in Holland, please write to *Penguin Books Nederland B.V., Postbus 195, NL-1380AD Weesp, Netherlands*.

In Germany: For a complete list of books available from Penguin, please write to *Penguin Books Ltd, Friedrichstrasse 10-12, D-6000 Frankfurt Main I, Federal Republic of Germany*.

In Spain: For a complete list of books available from Penguin in Spain, please write to *Longman, Penguin España, Calle San Nicolas 15, E-28013 Madrid, Spain*.

In Japan: For a complete list of books available from Penguin in Japan, please write to *Longman Penguin Japan Co Ltd, Yamaguchi Building, 2-12-9 Kanda Jimbocho, Chiyoda-Ku, Tokyo 101, Japan*.

FOR THE BEST IN CONTEMPORARY AMERICAN FICTION (🐧)

FOR THE BEST IN CONTEMPORARY AMERICAN FICTION ⊘

☐ **THE WOMEN OF BREWSTER PLACE**
A Novel in Seven Stories
Gloria Naylor

Winner of the American Book Award, this is the story of seven survivors of an urban housing project — a blind alley feeding into a dead end. From a variety of backgrounds, they experience, fight against, and sometimes transcend the fate of black women in America today.

192 pages   ISBN: 0-14-006690-X   **$5.95**

☐ **STONES FOR IBARRA**
Harriet Doerr

An American couple comes to the small Mexican village of Ibarra to reopen a copper mine, learning much about life and death from the deeply faithful villagers.   *214 pages   ISBN: 0-14-007562-3*   **$5.95**

☐ **WORLD'S END**
T. Coraghessan Boyle

"Boyle has emerged as one of the most inventive and verbally exuberant writers of his generation," writes *The New York Times*. Here he tells the story of Walter Van Brunt, who collides with early American history while searching for his lost father.   *456 pages   ISBN: 0-14-009760-0*   **$8.95**

☐ **THE WHISPER OF THE RIVER**
Ferrol Sams

The story of Porter Osborn, Jr., who, in 1938, leaves his rural Georgia home to face the world at Willingham University, *The Whisper of the River* is peppered with memorable characters and resonates with the details of place and time. Ferrol Sams's writing is regional fiction at its best.

528 pages   ISBN: 0-14-008387-1   **$6.95**

☐ **ENGLISH CREEK**
Ivan Doig

Drawing on the same heritage he celebrated in *This House of Sky,* Ivan Doig creates a rich and varied tapestry of northern Montana and of our country in the late 1930s.   *338 pages   ISBN: 0-14-008442-8*   **$6.95**

☐ **THE YEAR OF SILENCE**
Madison Smartt Bell

A penetrating look at the varied reactions to a young woman's suicide exactly one year later, *The Year of Silence* "captures vividly and poignantly the chancy dance of life." (*The New York Times Book Review*)

208 pages   ISBN: 0-14-011533-1   **$6.95**